UNDER THE
DOMIM TREE

To Den, Dicodidto
Lyla and all others.

UNDER THE DOMIM TREE

GILA ALMAGOR

TRANSLATED BY HILLEL SCHENKER

Simon & Schuster Books for Young Readers

Also by Gila Almagor:
The Summer of Aviya

 SIMON & SCHUSTER BOOKS FOR YOUNG READERS
An imprint of Simon & Schuster Children's Publishing Division
1230 Avenue of the Americas
New York, NY 10020
Text copyright © 1995 by Gila Almagor
All rights reserved including the right of reproduction in whole or
in part in any form.
Originally published in Israel in 1992 by Am Oved as Etz Hadomim Tafus.
SIMON & SCHUSTER BOOKS FOR YOUNG READERS is a trademark
of Simon & Schuster.
Designed by Virginia Pope.
The text of this book is set in Bembo.
Manufactured in the United States of America.

10 9 8 7 6 5 4 3 2 1

Library of Congress Cataloging-in-Publication Data
Almagor, Gila.
      ['Ets ha-domim tafus. English]
      Under the domim tree / by Gila Almagor ; Hillel Schenker, translator.
               p.   cm.
      Summary: Chronicles the joys and troubles experienced by a group
of teenagers, mostly Holocaust survivors, living at an Israeli youth settlement in
1953.
      [1. Holocaust survivors—Fiction. 2. Isreal—Fiction.
  3. Interpersonal relations—Fiction.] I. Schenker, Hillel. II. Title.
PZ7.A4451Un   1995   [Fic]—dc20   95-3356
ISBN: 0-671-89020-4

To my beloved Yankele and Hagar

—G. A.

INTRODUCTION

At the end of World War II, when the dimensions of the Holocaust became known, emissaries from Israel began the sacred task of seeking the Jewish children who survived amid the ruins of Europe. The children were discovered in basements and in forests, in granaries and in monasteries. Here and there, children were discovered hidden in the homes of non-Jewish people, people who later became known as "The Righteous Gentiles."

The surviving children were gathered together by the Israeli emissaries and placed in children's homes that were established for this purpose throughout Europe. There, the children were warmly received and were prepared for their immigration to Israel. In Israel, youth villages were built for these children, these rescued embers from the flames of Europe. One of the most important challenges facing the children who lived through the Holocaust, who were cut off from the homes of their mothers and fathers and torn away from the lands of their birth, was to strike new roots in the new land. Youth villages helped them do this.

There are still a few youth villages in Israel today. *Under the Domim Tree,* set in 1953, is based on my own experience of living in a youth village called Hadassim (named Udim in the novel), located on Israel's coastal plain.

Most youth villages are agricultural communities, similar to boarding schools. Many have grain crops, a cow shed, a sheep pen, chicken coops, vegetable and flower gardens, apple and citrus orchards, and even hand-icrafts, such as sewing and carpentry.

The children who live at these youth villages work in different branches, according to a set schedule over the course of a year. This creates a strong connection with the land and the country, and enables the children to learn work skills they can use as adults.

In addition to the crops and orchards that were an integral part of the youth village of my childhood, we were blessed with a very special tree—the domim tree. A familiar tree in our region, "domim" is the tree's Arabic name. In books that define the plants and flowers of Israel, it is called "Ziziphus-Spring-Christ" or the "Judas Tree." The domim tree has grown in Israel since biblical days, and it is mentioned a number of times in the Bible under the Hebrew name "sheizaf." It can be found in many different areas in Israel, in various sizes. Sometimes it's a tall tree with a thin, sturdy trunk. Sometimes the tree is shaped like a small sapling. It has shiny green leaves and blossoms once or twice a year, bearing sour fruit, which looks like little green apples.

The leaves on the domim tree of my youth almost never fell off, and the tree hardly bore any fruit. For us, and only for us, it was forever green, so that we could always come and find shelter in its shade.

To this day, I don't know who planted the domim tree in our youth village. Back then, we believed the tree planted itself and grew at the edge of a hill. No one watered it, and no one took care of it. But deep in our hearts, we believed that it quenched its thirst from our tears—the tears of children who came to cry and pour out their hearts, one by one, under its protective branches.

The youth village was the best home I ever had. I will always remember it as an island of goodness and beauty, made even more special by the domim tree.

—*Gila Almagor*

CHAPTER 1

I t all began one winter's day in the middle of the afternoon when Ariel, our counselor, decided to raise the issue of the German reparations. "Should the Israeli government accept or reject reparations from the German government for the Nazi crimes?" That's how he began. It was the first time that the subject of the Holocaust had been raised for discussion in our group. Until that day we hadn't spoken *here* about what had happened *there*—as if the past had been erased, as if everything began here, in Israel. Initially the discussion was very straightforward. The majority felt that there could be no reparations for genocide, for the murder of people, that money couldn't compensate for blood. I said, "Since I was born here, in Israel, I feel that I have no right to express an opinion about what happened there."

At first it was hard to recognize the storm that was brewing in the hearts of the kids. But later, in the dining room, Sarah B. said, "I don't believe the stupidity that I heard this afternoon. You're all thinking like little

children. After all, we're immigrants; we don't have parents who will look after us and do our thinking for us.
We're talking about money. About the future. About our
future. My future. I know that I deserve compensation. I
know that they won't return my parents to me, or my
family, or the childhood that they stole from me. But
finally, I will have something that is mine."

Daniel shouted at her, "What kind of person are you?
We're talking about our people, about the government of
Israel, and you are trying to turn it into a personal dis-
cussion!"

"Is that anything new?" Zevick said. "Sarah was always
different, an individualist. Why are you surprised? Don't
waste your words or your nerves, Daniel. Just listen to
how she talks: 'My future. My family.' As if we all didn't
come from the same place!"

Zevick kept rubbing it in. "Just look at her, Daniel.
Look at what she's eating. Gang," he continued, encouraged by the silence that had spread across the dining
room. "Look at her." And everyone looked and laughed,
releasing the tension that had been accumulating since
the discussion on the reparations had begun. Zevick
wouldn't stop: "Look, look at what she's eating. She's eating matzoh in the middle of the year. She's been saving
it ever since Passover, because she's on a diet, and God
forbid that she should run out of matzoh. She's not like
all the other fat and simple girls in our group."

When he said the words "fat and simple," voices
attacked him from all sides. "Come on, Zevick, stop

insulting us. There are some really beautiful girls in our group."

Others cried out, "More! More!"

Zevick just continued his lecture. "Where was I? Oh yes, Sarah B. She's different. She's *special.*" And he cut up the word "special" into three syllables, emphasizing every sound—*spe-ci-al.*

Once again all eyes turned toward Sarah B. Everyone was waiting to see how she would react. And then we saw her chewing away at her matzoh, which was practically stuck in her throat.

She began to cough, and pieces of matzoh flew out of her mouth and scattered around the table. She no longer looked like a lady. Sarah B. tried to say something, but her voice was gone; her face was turning red, she began waving her hands, and she looked like someone who was drowning in the sea, struggling against the waves. Naomi, her good friend who was sitting next to her, hit her back and gave her a glass of water. Only then did the coughing stop. "Zevick, take a look at yourself," Sarah said in a hoarse voice. "You're so filled with envy. You'd just love to look a little different. You're so unkempt. So unfortunate. So from *there!* So like you just got off the boat. Do I look like I just got off the boat? Everyone thinks I was born here, in Israel. If you were a human being, maybe I'd offer you my matzoh, but you're nothing, Zevick, just Yurek's little servant. That's all you've ever been."

That was a real deathblow. Sarah's last words really

took Zevick by surprise. He looked over at Yurek, who was sitting there quietly.

"Did you hear what she said, Yurek?" he asked. "I'm nothing? I'm from *there*?" He waited to see what Yurek would do, and then he sat down mumbling, "There's no one to talk to, no one."

And then Yurek got up. "Leave Zevick alone, okay?" There was silence, nobody spoke, and then a minute later Yurek continued, "Sarah, I want to understand something. What do you mean by 'My money. My future'? Your future is the same as ours—the group, the training farm, and the kibbutz that we'll begin. Don't you think that's a good enough future?"

Sarah B. looked at him and responded in a confident voice, "Yurek, you make me laugh. Do you really think that I'm planning my future with all of you? With this group? We've been together for seven years, ever since the war. That's plenty of time. Enough. I want to be able to get up in the morning alone and to go to sleep alone, in my own room and not together with four other girls. I don't want a group; I don't want to live with all of you for the rest of my life. Do you understand me, Yurek?" All of us were tense, waiting to see how he would react.

This time, Yurek, who always had a quick response to everything, was silent. He just stared at Sarah B. with a penetrating gaze. His narrowed eyes looked even narrower; his Adam's apple stood out even more than usual, and it moved as if he were talking. But he didn't say a word.

Sarah B. knew exactly what to do with that moment. She had an audience, and the stage was all hers. "So you're silent, Yurek? Have nothing to say? You're just not used to someone thinking differently, and saying it to your face—particularly me, huh?"

The eerie silence that spread over the dining room was broken by Ariel. "Gang," he said, "I understand all the excitement. It was to be expected that different opinions would be heard. The whole country has been in turmoil for months over the question of the German reparations, and we'll be returning to the subject again and again. But as for this, I must say that I admire Sarah's honesty and courage." He didn't call her Sarah B. We called her that, so as not to confuse her with Sarah Altman, whom we called Sarah A. "I hope," he continued, "that you'll learn how to listen to an individual opinion and how to respect it." We didn't like the sympathetic tone in his voice when he spoke about Sarah B. Yurek was the unofficial leader of our group. And he had been defeated by Sarah B., his girlfriend, and Ariel even expressed an understanding for her.

Before Ariel had finished speaking, Yurek had gotten up and left the dining room. At first we thought it was just for a moment, that he would be right back. But when he didn't return, Zevick said, "The monster ruined his appetite."

During the meal I prepared sandwiches of white cheese, olives, tomato, and lettuce for Yurek, and I wrapped them up in a napkin. Before we left, I gave the sandwiches to Zevick. "They're for Yurek," I said.

"When are you going to stop worrying about the whole world?" my best friend, Ayala, asked me. "Let his girlfriend make food for him."

On the following day we continued arguing until evening, and the storm still hadn't subsided. At the entrance to the dining room, I was just washing my hands in the sink when I bumped into Yurek. He was standing right next to me. "Clean hands? Let's see," he said. I obediently stretched out my hands and almost touched him. He tossed a ball of paper into my out-stretched palms and said, "It's for you, Aviya."

"Thanks," I said, and turned toward my table. I thought, *This Yurek, he doesn't thank me for yesterday's sand-wiches, but he gives me a ball of paper.* So why did I blush when he stood so close to me? I hoped that he hadn't noticed how excited I was. When he spoke to me, I felt his words blowing in my face. He had never stood so close to me before.

And then, at that exact moment, Sarah B. came in and sat down at her regular place at Yurek's table. They always sat together. They were going together. A couple. The oldest and most stable couple in our group. Two that were one. Even when they had arrived at the youth vil-lage, directly from Poland, from *there,* they were already a couple.

I came to the village after they did, and they were introduced to me as Sarah B., who's going with Yurek,

and Yurek, who's going with Sarah B. But this time, the
moment she sat down next to him, Yurek got up.
Without saying a word, he moved over to the next table,
even though all the places were already taken. So everyone crowded together, and Yurek squeezed in among
them. Even when he and Sarah B. argued in the past,
Yurek had never gone to another table like that.
Normally when things were tough for him, he would
get up and leave the room without touching his food, as
he had the previous evening. So we were all curious to
see what was going to happen and how Sarah B. would
react.

Yurek, with his usual calm, picked up a slice of bread
and began to chew on it, as if he were the only one in
the small dining room with its six tables. Finally Sarah B.
said, "Look at him. Since yesterday he hasn't said a word
to me. He's trying to avoid me because I have a different
opinion about something, and I dared to say what I
think." Yurek continued to eat as if he hadn't heard her,
and Sarah B. continued, "You've got a problem, Yurek?
You're not used to it? You just can't comprehend the—"

She hadn't even finished the sentence when a rum-
ble of voices was heard, "Comprehend . . . wow . . . what
language, Sarah B., . . . great Hebrew!"

Then Zevick said out loud, "To comprehend! All of
you should learn how to speak good Hebrew from Lady
Sarah."

Sarah began to shout over the noises of laughter and
disdain, "Go ahead and laugh! But even my Hebrew is

better than yours. We'll see who laughs last."

Just as she was about to continue her lecture to
Yurek, he got up, came over to our table, and said to me,
"Come with me for a second."

"Who, me?" I said surprised.

"Yes," he said. "I'm speaking to you, aren't I?"

Ayala kicked me in the knee and whispered, "Go
ahead, Aviya. He's calling you." And I, like a good disci-
plined girl, got up and amidst all the uproar in the dining
room, nobody noticed that we went out together. Or
maybe they did, but nobody said anything.

Near the row of sinks at the entrance to the dining
room, he stopped and asked, "Well, did you read it?"

"Read what?" I asked.

"The letter."

"What letter? I didn't get any letter."

"But I gave it to you, right here, near the sink. I gave
you a letter."

"Come on, Yurek; don't make fun of me," I said. "You
gave me a ball of paper, not a letter."

He looked me straight in the eye and said, "Oh, no, I
hope you didn't throw it away."

Confused, I answered, "No, it's here in my pocket."

I took the ball of paper out of my pocket, and when
I started to give it to him, he grabbed my hand and com-
manded, "Read it!"

Just then Zevick appeared and asked, "What happened?"

Yurek said, "Is she still talking in there? I can't stand

the sound of her voice." And then they went back into the dining room.

I rushed into the bathroom and hid in one of the stalls. By the pale light of the lantern I unraveled the ball of paper, straightened it out as best I could, and pressed it against the white tiled wall. The paper was very crumpled, and I could barely make out the handwriting.

"To you," it said at the top of the page, not "Dear" or "Hello." Just "To you." He didn't continue with my name, but with "I really liked what you said yesterday in the discussion about the German reparations. That's exactly what I hope to hear from a *sabra*, a native Israeli who wasn't there. You know, I really like to listen to you. 'Since I was born here, I feel that I have no right to express an opinion about what happened there.' I'll always remember that sentence. And your voice, too ... " A word was erased, and then he wrote, "I think we have a lot to talk about, and if you want, I'll wait for you behind the kitchen after dinner." And on a separate line, he wrote, "P.S.—(1) It's over with Sarah B., and that's final. (2) Thanks for those sandwiches yesterday. (3) Never cut off your braid, ever. It's really beautiful." At the bottom of the page, it said, "From me," with an unclear signature.

I was totally astounded. I read the letter over and over again. At first I thought he was pulling my leg, making fun of me. That would suit him. Yurek did things like that, practical jokes. Every so often, he would find a new victim and have fun at that person's expense. But why me? Why now?

Like most of the girls in the group, I was secretly in love with Yurek, though none of us really had a chance, since he was Sarah B.'s Yurek. But maybe, after yesterday's argument, he had decided to break off from her?

I returned to the dining room, snuck a look at him, and thought he turned the other way. Once again I felt a loss of confidence and was sure that it was all just a practical joke. *He might be setting a trap for you*, I warned myself. So I decided to ignore the letter and everything that had come before it.

Immediately after I sat down at my table, Rachel, the youth village principal, came in with short, determined steps. She suddenly stopped, shocked by all of the fuss going on in the dining room. Waving her little hands around, she tried to silence us. "What happened to your manners? Did you forget that you're in the dining room?"

Ariel got up from his seat and approached her. "I want to apologize, Rachel. There's been an argument going on here since yesterday about the German reparations."

Zevick shouted, "There's no argument! Except for Sarah B., everyone else agrees, more or less."

"You don't have to shout, Zevick," Rachel said. "I also hear when people speak quietly." Then Rachel turned to Ariel, whispered something to him, and they both left.

My friend Ayala took advantage of that moment to ask me, "Where did you disappear to?"

"To the bathroom," I answered.

But she wouldn't give up. "You went out with Yurek. What did he want?" But before I could answer, Ariel and Rachel came back, accompanied by a girl. It was "the new girl." She had come. In the middle of the year, in the middle of supper—it was really bad timing.

We had all been new at this youth village once and had experienced the difficulties. We knew that it was best to come to a village at the beginning of the year, because then you were just one of a whole bunch of new pupils. It's also good to come toward the end of the year, because by the beginning of the following year, you would already be known and wouldn't be considered a greenhorn. But this one, she showed up so suddenly, right in the middle of supper.

Ariel called out to us, "Hey, guys, I need your attention for a moment." The noise continued, and Ariel raised his voice: "Quiet!" As the ruckus died down, he said with warmth, "Gang, I want to introduce you to a new girl who is joining our group. This is Miriam."

The new girl cut in and said, "Mira!"

Ariel was clearly surprised. "What did you say?"

"Mira. My name is Mira."

There was a moment of confusion before Ariel continued. "Excuse me, I'm sorry. So this is Mira." He looked at her as if to get her confirmation and then added, "And I hope you all help her to get adjusted and to feel at home with us." He glanced around the dining room, surveyed all the tables, and his eyes stopped at our table. "Mira, this evening you'll join the vegetarian table, and tomorrow we'll find you another place. Maybe you're a vegetarian?" She said that she wasn't, and Ariel accompanied her to our table.

There were five vegetarians in our group. "The rabbits' table" is what they called our table, because of the mountains of lettuce and carrots that were always piled in front of us. Before Ariel sat Mira down, he told us, "Girls, after the meal ends take Mira to your room. She'll sleep in the empty lower bed, the one that belonged to Dita." And then he introduced all of us who were sitting around the table.

Mira sat down and immediately said, "How come I don't have any chicken?"

Daniel answered, "This is a vegetarian table."

She seemed to ignore him. "But I don't eat grass," she protested. We were dumbfounded. After all, she was new. She had just arrived in the middle of the meal. What did she expect? That we would be waiting for her with the regular food she was used to?

Ayala kicked my knee, our elbows touched, we exchanged glances, and immediately we knew that we didn't like her. From the moment she joined our table till the end of dinner, we didn't exchange a single word with her.

Throughout the entire meal, Yurek didn't glance at me even once. I actually dared to look straight at him one time. But he was speaking, and everyone around his table was listening.

I wanted to know what he was talking about, so I got up and went over to Zevick, who was our group's work coordinator. I asked him if there was any change in tomorrow's work schedule, and Zevick looked at me strangely. "No, why should there be? Until Wim comes back from Holland, there won't be any changes." Wim was our gardener. I was standing right next to Yurek, but he didn't even bat an eyelash. I returned to my table and was now convinced that the letter was just a joke. If I showed up behind the kitchen to meet him, he would just laugh at me. Yurek was perfectly capable of hiding behind the bushes near the kitchen together with Zevick and Daniel and mocking me when I arrived. And why should he want me of all people anyway? Besides his own Sarah B., there were a lot of girls in our group who were prettier than me, particularly those who he knew *there*, in Poland, so there was that special relationship between them. They really had a bond, a closeness. Ayala and I frequently talked about it.

We were born in Israel, the only two sabras in our group. We often felt like two strangers who just happened to find themselves by accident in the group. They never said a bad word about us, no negative comments at our expense, but still, we were different. Sure, we all looked very similar. We dressed almost alike, and our clothes came from the same clothing dispensary, but there was a marked difference in the way we spoke. They still had trouble with Hebrew, with the rolling of the letter *resh*, the r sound, and they still had foreign manners that filtered into their daily behavior. It was hard to put a finger on it, but there was a sort of sense of "them" and "us."

When the new girl, Mira, joined us at the table, I tried to figure out where she was from. *Here* or *there*. In our group we never said the words "Poland," "Holocaust," or even "home." Those words were forbidden. It's not as if anyone banned them, but they were never mentioned. Anyone who came from that terrible war was from *there*. And we, Ayala and I, two native-born Israeli sabras, were from *here*.

Like parts in a puzzle, I tried to find parts of Mira's past in her face, but her face was a mystery and didn't reveal a thing. She looked just like us. She wore heavy brown shoes, dark blue pants, a white shirt, and a dark blue sweater with a zipper in front. But unlike us she also wore a blue farmer's cap. That strange hat, why did she wear it in the evening? And why didn't she take it off during the meal? It gave her a really strange expression. It cast a shadow over half her face and hid her eyes. And an army knapsack was always laying on her knees. I almost told her to put it down on the floor so that she could eat comfortably, but when she started complaining about the food, I lost any desire I had to make an effort to be nice and to try to make things easier for her. There was something about her that seemed to be broadcast to us from the very first moment: "Don't come near me; I'm not interested!"

At the end of the meal, Ariel came back to our table and said, "Mira, you're in good hands, the best. These two will really help you." And to us he said, "I hope you'll get along."

CHAPTER 2

On the way out of the dining room, Ayala said to Mira, "Didn't you forget your suitcase?"

"It's all here," Mira said, pointing to the knapsack that was hanging over her shoulder.

When we got to the room, we pulled out Dita's lower bed. Ayala looked at me. "You know, I suddenly miss her." I was silent. "Don't you miss her?"

"Yes, sure," I replied, but I wasn't really thinking about Dita at that moment.

Afterward, we explained to Mira how to open the lower bed and how to fold it and put it back in its place in the morning. "Why do I have to fold it every morning?" Mira asked. "It can stand in the room throughout the day just like all the other beds. No one takes advantage of me! I'm no sucker!" *A sucker? What sort of expression is that?* I thought. Without exchanging a word with Ayala, it was clear to both of us that it was best not to respond, to hold it in—otherwise, one of us might explode.

There was something really upsetting about Mira; it was as if she were always looking for a fight. Her coarse language was foreign to us. And if she hadn't suddenly asked about Dita, we would have just left her alone in the room and gone out. "So where's the girl who was here before me?" she asked. We told her she was called Dita, and that her mother had gotten married and had taken her to America.

Ayala added provocatively, "To a millionaire. She married a millionaire."

Mira repeated with disdain, "I bet. A millionaire."

"You don't believe it? You want to see a picture?" Ayala challenged. And without waiting for an answer, she showed Mira the picture that stood next to the little glass vase near her bed. "Here, look. This is her mother's house. Only millionaires have a house like that. It's huge. And look at the garden, it's beautiful."

It was a color picture, the first time I had ever seen a color picture. "And in natural colors," Ayala added. "Did you ever see a picture like this, in natural colors?" Green grass surrounded the house, and it was decorated with flowers everywhere. "And this is Dita, our friend. Just look at her clothes and her new bike." We pointed to the blue bike, decorated with all sorts of special gadgets, which to us was really an extraordinary sight. "Well, now do you believe us?" Ayala asked, and waited for an answer.

Mira didn't respond. Ayala continued, "And the presents that she sends us. You've never seen anything like

them." She took the funny shining socks that Dita had
sent in the last package from America out of her drawer in the chest, as well as the green and pink ballpoint
pens. No one in our youth village had pens like that.
"And here are the candies. Go ahead, taste them,"
offered Ayala, taking one of them out of the colored box
and putting it in her mouth. Mira took a handful of
candy out of the box, put two of them into her mouth,
and the rest into her pants pocket. We were stunned.
Ayala had just said "taste them," but Mira took a whole
handful! When Ayala offered me some of her candies, I
refused to accept them. Candy was a rarity at our youth
village, and on the few occasions that we had any, we ate
them one at a time, very slowly, so that they would last
forever. All of the girls in the room received an identical
package from Dita, and we took care not to eat from one
another's box.

Despite Ayala's shock, she continued to try to be nice
to Mira. "In America, the people actually throw candy at
all their favorite singers. That's what Dita says. She tells us
everything about America."

Mira didn't understand. "If they love the singers, why
do they throw candy at them?" she asked. For a moment
I thought she had a point and was about to tell her so,
but I decided not to. Ayala put the candy back in its
place. When she put the picture next to the vase, Mira
said, "This Dita, she must have been pretty stupid. How
could she have agreed to this arrangement? I wouldn't
have agreed to sleep in the lower pullout bed."

We were really losing our patience, but still, we explained to her that at the beginning of every year, we drew lots to see who got which bed and which drawers, and that was that. Every room had a lower pullout bed, and someone had to get it. "And you arrived so suddenly," we told her, "in the middle of the year and everything, so it's the only bed left." Afterward we showed her her drawer, and Ayala explained how the room duties worked: Each girl was on duty for a full week. She had to wash the floor, make sure that there were fresh flowers in the vases, and put the mail that arrived in the appropriate drawers. Not very complicated or difficult.

Ayala kept talking, but I was still thinking only of Yurek. I wondered if he had gone to the meeting place. *Is he waiting for me?* I asked myself. *Did I do the right thing when I didn't go? Maybe the arrival of this new girl has really messed things up for me?*

Just then there was a knock on the door, and when I opened it, I saw Yurek standing there. I was surprised, and I knew that my thoughts had brought him to me. "I want to ask you something," he said, and I felt my face turning red.

Ayala stared at me with her big eyes, as if she were saying, "Go to him. He's waiting for you." I left the room.

"Why didn't you come?" he asked. "I've been waiting for you." When he spoke he looked me straight in the eye, and I was just beaming inside. He came. He

waited for me. He didn't even hesitate to come to my
room and be seen with me.

Quietly I said, "I came. Here I am." We walked side
by side, not saying a word, and when we arrived behind
the kitchen I said, "You see? I came to the exact place
that you suggested." And while we were still standing
among the bushes behind the kitchen, Martha, the cook,
came out to throw some garbage into the giant cans that
were filled with leftovers and rotting vegetables.

She noticed us and called out in her thundering
voice, "Who's there? What do you want with the
garbage? You didn't have enough to eat? Get out of
here!" Holding in our laughter, we ran away as fast as we
could, and without having planned it, made our way
toward the hill.

We entered the path that led toward the domim tree.
Yurek was walking ahead of me, and I could make out
his golden curls waving in the wind and his sharp fea-
tures. It began to rain. Yurek said, "Do you mind getting
a little wet, or are you made of sugar and want to go
back?"

"I like the rain," I answered. But I was cold, and my
wet clothes began sticking to my skin. Just like Yurek, I
lifted my head, and tried to swallow the rain and let it
wash my face.

By the time the rain stopped, we had reached the
edge of the hill that overlooked our youth village and all
the settlements in the vicinity, whose lights sparkled like
stars in the night. We stood under the domim tree, with

raindrops still dripping off its leaves. "I love to come here at night," Yurek said. "During the day, everyone's always waiting in line to come up here, but at night, at this hour, the tree is all mine." And then he came close to me and spoke softly. "Could you open up your braid?" I unraveled the braid. Yurek looked at me. "Nice," he said. "Your hair is beautiful." Then he ran his fingers through my hair, and I felt his fingertips. I trembled and didn't want him to stop. He covered my face with my hair, uncovered it, and covered it again. For a moment he started to say something, but then he changed his mind. I was silent, totally obsessed with the touch of his hand. After a long silence, I heard him say, "My sister, she also had them." He continued uttering broken sentences. "She had...braids...long...long..." I wanted him to say more, to tell me. "I had a sister, an older sister, and also a brother," he said. Later, after a long silence, Yurek asked, "Where are you from in Israel?"

"From a bad place," I said.

"I've never been there; don't know it," he said with a twinkle in his eye. "Actually, I've hardly been anyplace in Israel. Maybe we could take a trip some time. You could show me your city."

"My little town," I corrected him. "It's just a very small town. And you? Where are you from?"

"From *there*," he said. "You know, I'm from *there*." A moment later he added, "It's almost lights-out time. We have to get back." We went down the hill on the same path we came up on. That was the first time that I ever went up and down on the same path.

There were two paths on the hill. One went up, and the other went down. We children from the youth village had created these paths with our feet. As time went on, there was an unspoken rule: You go up the hill on the path that leads from the road, and you go down on the other side. As you start going down, whoever is next in line starts going up toward the domim tree. But Yurek and I broke the rule.

We made our way down the muddy, slippery path. When I slipped and fell, Yurek grabbed me by the arm. "I'm here; I'll take care of you. Don't worry," he assured me. When we reached the main road, Yurek said, "Your braid, fix it."

"Braid it," I said. "You don't *fix* a braid, you *braid* it."

"Thank you, teacher," he said. "So braid it, please, and try to get dry so that you won't catch a cold. I need you."

Yurek doesn't need anyone—that's what we always said about him behind his back. We talked about him a lot. And now, I had heard him say, "I need you." When we parted near the girls' quarters, Yurek pulled my braid. "Are you my girlfriend?" he asked. "Are we going together?"

I repeated after him, "Together."

"No," he said, "I want to hear you say it. Say 'I'm Yurek's girlfriend.'" When I spoke, he looked at the movement of my lips, as if he were trying to understand something. "How do you do it?" he asked. "That *resh*, the rolling 'r.' Teach me how to say the Hebrew letter *resh* like that. My *resh* sounds like it's from *there*, like I'm a new immigrant."

"I'll teach you, Yurek," I said. Actually, I liked his strange rolling *resh* and his foreign mannerisms. He held out his hand. For a moment I hesitated, and his hand remained hanging in the air. Then I stretched out my hand and shook his extended palm. I felt as if a pact had been sealed between us. We were going together! I turned and ran toward my room.

The room was empty; all the girls had gone to take a shower. So I was able to calm down from all the excitement. I could hardly wait to write in my diary, which was hidden in its regular place under my mattress. Before I went to take a shower, I put my hand under the mattress, felt the diary, and heard myself saying, "Soon we're going to meet, my friend! Wait for me here. You won't regret it. I've got a lot to tell you tonight." Then I went to the showers.

When I waded in through the clouds of steam, hardly anyone noticed me. I was able to avoid having to explain why my clothes were damp and my hair wet, and where I was coming from at such a late hour. The girls had already taken over all the sinks, and I was forced to wait until one became available. I spread my towel over the moist wooden bench that stood next to the white porcelain wall. I sat there and looked at them, my friends who were just like me, no longer girls, not yet women. I knew them well. We had already been together for a

number of years. Eating, sleeping, and taking showers.
Without embarrassment, without shame, like sisters in
one big family. And yet, I didn't really *know* them. Their
past was a mystery to me. I loved to look at them and to
try to guess what it was like for them *there*. What do they
remember? What are they running from?

I really loved that evening hour in the showers. It was
the center of our life. We laughed a lot, gossiped about the
boys, and allowed ourselves the luxury of doting on ourselves. The crowning example of this was Sarah B.'s daily
ritual. We all followed every step of the facial that she gave
herself, which began at the end of the meal, when she
took a little bit of margarine from the table and wrapped
it in a paper napkin. When she reached the shower room,
Sarah B. would begin to prepare: Pieces of cotton, her
hair brush, and her margarine were all placed within easy
reach. Her good friend Naomi, who always did everything for her, would drag a chair from their room, all the
way to the showers. She'd spread out a towel, and Sarah
B. would climb up onto the chair, after Naomi had wiped
the steam from the mirror. Sarah B. would look at herself,
carefully examining her body. As she climbed down from
the chair she used to mumble to herself, "Good girl,
Sarah'le," calling herself by her nickname with a lot of
self-love and admiration. "That's the way, that's the way."
Then she'd begin her facial treatment. She'd rub on the
margarine and then tap her face lightly with her long fingers. When she was finished, it was time for the massage.

She would massage her forehead, her cheeks, and her

chin in slow, circular movements, with the confidence of
an expert, and then she would slowly brush her black,
wavy hair. She'd bend forward, her face toward the floor,
and she'd run the brush over her hair, stroking and
counting. One hundred twenty times she would brush
her hair. And while she was counting, it was impossible
to interrupt her. If anyone tried to talk to her, she'd
respond with a shake of her head or a wave of her free
hand, and she'd continue to brush and count: "eighty,
eighty-one, eighty-two..." until she reached one hundred twenty. Sarah B. had patience, and she also had
discipline. How did she know all of this? Who taught her
what to do and how to do it? She had no family.

Most of the girls in our group had a relative here and
a relative there, who kept contact with them and even
invited them to visit from time to time. But Sarah B.,
even on holidays and vacations, stayed behind at the
youth village. She had no place to go. Together with
Yurek, Daniel, Eli, Alex, and Zevick, she would wander
around the grounds like a dog that had been abandoned
in a huge backyard. When we would leave, filled with
excitement, for our monthly holiday outside the youth
village, they would always act as if they couldn't wait for
us to leave, for the school to empty out and leave them
alone.

And when we returned from the holiday, Sarah B.
would say, "Why did you come back so quickly? We had
such a great time here without you." Naomi would
always bring Sarah B. something from her aunt's house,

a little present. Compensation for the fact that she had to
stay behind. Naomi's loyalty to Sarah B. was really something. And Sarah B. responded in kind. In the eighth
grade, toward the end of elementary school, when
Naomi failed her class and there was a danger that she
would be left back and wouldn't be able to be together
with us in the high school, Sarah B. went out of her way
to help her. When Naomi's marks began to improve, we
all knew why. We didn't like her, Sarah B. There was
something stuck-up about her. In her thinking, she was
older than us, and her body was more developed. She
was almost a woman. Yet deep inside of me I admired her
personality and her special character.

While I was still watching all the girls, leaning over
the sinks, washing their clothes, Yola began to quietly
hum a strange melody. Sarah B. joined her, and as others
joined in, the quiet hum became the beautiful sound of
song. They sang in a wonderful two-part harmony, and
suddenly Yola stopped and said, "You know, in Poland, it's
bez time now. The *bez* leaves are falling."

"What do you mean, it's *bez* now, Yola?" Sarah A.
asked. "What month is it?"

"It's the Hebrew month of *Shvat*," Yola said.

"No, no," said Sarah A. "What month is it in Poland?"

"February," someone offered.

Yola added dreamily, "Yes, February is *bez*, and when
you walk in the forest and step on the leaves they go
creeek, creeek, creeek."

But Sarah A. didn't agree. "What do you mean, *creeek,*

creeek, creeek? They go *chack, chack, chack.* And who says it
happens in February? The *bez* tree leaves fall off in
October, in the fall. February? In February, everything is
completely covered with snow, up to here." She pointed
to the top of the sink. "And when you step on the snow,
it makes no sound at all."

This conversation, about a *bez*, which I had never
heard of, went on and on. Ayala and I were, of course,
silent. I looked around and saw before me little girls from
another place, in another time, little girls who were
walking in a dense forest filled with multitudes of whispering leaves and sounds that I had never heard. All of
those longings and yearnings for home, for father and
mother, for nature, for voices, for colors, for everything
that was there, were channeled into the sound of those
leaves that were once under their little feet covered with
warm winter shoes. Their bodies were covered and well
protected against the cold weather, and Yurek, who suddenly broke into my thoughts, yes Yurek was there too: a
little boy, with bright blond hair, dressed in a strange
heavy coat, in the middle of the big forest, walking and
laughing, sure of himself, skipping among the *bez* leaves
that fell from the trees and went *creeek, creeek,* or *chack,
chack.* I noticed that Yola was wiping away a tear with her
soapy hands. "I got some soap in my eyes," she said. "It
always happens to me."

The singing continued, and I hoped that this
moment would never end. And then, Mira, the new girl,
came in and broke the magic spell. "What is this, don't

you have a laundry at this place? What are you doing
standing there like washer women in the middle of the
night?"

We explained to her that there was a laundry, but the
personal things, like her underwear and her bras, she had
to do on her own. "It's private, it's yours," we said. "At
least that's how we do it."

The singing stopped, the clouds of steam disappeared, and the magic was gone. The shower room began
to empty out, and I remained standing next to the sink,
washing my underwear. And out of the corner of my
eye, I saw Mira take off her clothes. I saw a scar on her
right shoulder and another one on the lower part of her
back. She caught my glance. "What are you staring at?"
she asked.

A little confused, I stammered, "No, I was…just…
daydreaming."

Back in the room I did everything slowly, trying to
gain time, hoping that by the time I finished all the lights
would be out and I'd be able to have a private ren-
dezvous with my diary in the bathroom. In the hallway
the nightly "pregnancy parade" had begun. Every night,
as soon as the lights went out, the march toward the
bathroom would begin. Everyone who kept a diary
would hide it in their pajama tops, so we all looked preg-
nant. We pretended that we had to run to the bathroom,
though actually, all we wanted was to just find a private
place to write. There, in the smallest, narrowest cubicles,
we wrote our deepest thoughts. The diary was our most

important treasure, and we always abided by the unwritten rule: Never try to read anyone else's diary.

When my turn came, I went into the cubicle, knelt down, and with the closed toilet seat serving as my desk, I wrote. I told my diary everything. About the new girl who had arrived so suddenly and about the argument that afternoon. About the reparations from Germany and about Yurek and the fears and happiness that accompanied his entrance into my life. And I concluded with a question: "Will he really be mine?" To this I added a long, long line of question marks, which reached to the end of the page.

When I got back to the dark room, the girls were sleeping. I returned my diary to its place under my mattress, kissed the picture of my father that was inside a brown envelope, and then I heard Ayala whisper, "What took you so long?"

"I don't know," I answered. "I'm still not sure what's happening." I curled up under the blanket and pulled it over my head. It was hot, really suffocating, and I could barely breathe, but finally, I was protected and cut off from the girls in the room, from disgusting Mira, from the whole world. At last I was alone!

CHAPTER 3

T hat night the silence was shattered by the threatening sound of wolves. Despite the fact that there were no wolves in the area, we knew that sound very well. We used to be awakened by those strange, shrill cries, drag ourselves out of our warm beds, and cling—still half asleep—to the window. There, we stared at two boys, Alex and Misha, as they ran in circles around the courtyard of the youth village making wolf noises. Alex was the older one, and he used to carry Misha on his back. The two of them galloped wildly, screaming and wailing in the night. We couldn't make out their exact figures. But their shadows resembled a monster with a huge hunchback, spurting forth streams of blue smoke. We would stand in total silence, watching that horrible sight. No one dared to turn on the light. And we knew that behind the other darkened windows stood the rest of the kids, just like us, watching with fear and trepidation.

This time the silence was broken by Mira. "Why are you all stuck there, frozen stiff? We've got to stop it right

away." She was about to open the window when Ayala
pushed her away.

And then when Mira went to turn the light on, Esty
rushed over, grabbed her hand, and warned, "Don't you
dare, do you hear me?"

Mira raised her voice. "No one shouts at me, and no
one touches me. And don't you forget it!" We stood
there, facing her, ready for a fight.

"Girls, don't answer her," Ayala said. "You can see
what she's like." And the truth was, at that late hour, we
really didn't want to argue. Our attention was totally
focused on Alex and Misha. At the end of their strange
ritual, Alex always took the boy down from his back, and
the terrifying monster would vanish, as if it had never
been there in the first place.

Then Alex brought Misha back to the boys' quarters.
It was only after we saw them disappear into the rooms
that we left the window and returned to sit silently on
our beds. A weight hung over the room. Mira's presence
had begun to annoy us. She had only just arrived, and
already, something had changed. Our room had really
been a positive example of togetherness. We never
argued. It was clean and well taken care of, and we loved
it. The main thing was that we had learned how to live
together harmoniously. And now, this one had come, and
she had brought with her a bad spirit.

We sat there for over an hour, but just couldn't fall
asleep. Esty and Chavi, who had known both Alex and
Misha back in Poland, began talking. "How many years

has this been going on already? And how come no one's
been able to help them?"

"If you want to talk, do it outside," Mira complained.
"I want to sleep."

The four of us left the room with our thick, woolen
blankets wrapped around us and went to sit on the
bench in the shower room. Slowly, one at a time, girls
from the other rooms began to join us. We looked like a
flock of nuns, crowded together, and the echo of our
voices whispered through the shower room like a silent
prayer. Someone quietly said, "What will happen to
them, to Alex and Misha? After all, one day they will
leave this youth village. How will they manage? They
just won't be able to live apart from each other."

And then we remembered that there had once been
an attempt to separate them. When the new psycholo-
gist, Dr. Alma Rothstein, arrived, she decided to liberate
them from their mutual dependency. One morning she
sent Misha to another youth village, and on that very
same day, Alex disappeared. He fled without leaving a
trace. We were all released from our studies and work,
and we joined in the search to find him. A day later we
heard that Misha had run away from the other village
and that they were looking for him, too. People even
came from there to look for him at our village. We
looked and looked but found nothing, as if the earth had
swallowed them up. Even the police joined the search,
which went on for days. We were petrified. And we were
afraid to talk about it, because we didn't dare dwell on

the cause of our fears. Then Dr. Rothstein vanished from our lives, just as abruptly as she had arrived.

The rumor about Misha and Alex's disappearance began to spread. Our neighbors in the immediate vicinity joined the search and scoured the whole area, armed with copies of their pictures. Alex's picture was terrible. His handsome face looked angry and tough. "Like an escaped criminal," someone said. We didn't even laugh.

The search parties spread out into the fields and the orange groves, a lot of people moving slowly. Hardly a voice was heard, except for the police, who every so often shouted into their megaphones, "Alexander Deutsch. The youth Alexander Deutsch. Give us a sign of life. Moshe Zinger, the child Moshe. Misha Zinger. We're looking for you. Don't be afraid. We only want what's good for you." Their calls resounded throughout the neighborhood, and the echoes followed their voices, and then there was silence once again. We held our breath and listened to every rustle of grass. Do they hear us? Will one of them give us a sign? The sight of people disappearing among the trees, and then reappearing, seemed to be straight out of a silent film. People were constantly scurrying around, without saying a word. There was just a constant fear that filled the air.

At the end of the second day, Ariel prepared us for a visit from the police's investigating officer. "He'll ask you about a lot of details that you probably know. Please don't hesitate to answer, because every detail might help." The officer arrived, together with two other policemen. They searched Alex's room, his drawer, among his clothes, and under his mattress. They took a few things and then gathered all of us together in the big activity room. The officer spoke, and one of the policemen kept notes all the time. He asked us to speak more slowly, so that he could keep up.

And then, for the first time, I heard Alex and Misha's story. Chavi, one of my roommates, did most of the talking. It was hard for her to talk; she was always so quiet. But the officer encouraged her, and in a weak voice, with her eyes to the ground, she explained: "They were neighbors. They lived in the same house in Kishinev, in Poland. One night the Germans came and took their parents away, and both of them managed to escape. For a long time they hid in the forest. In order to survive at night, they learned how to imitate the sounds of the wolves. At the end of the war, they were discovered in the forest, behaving like animals. A short while later, they were brought to Israel, to our youth village."

When Chavi finished, one of the kids added, "You should know that they have no relatives, nobody. No one has ever written to them or visited them." That was all anyone knew.

For four days we searched for them, and in the evenings, the police and the older people from the neighborhood came to continue the search, armed with giant flashlights and search dogs. Those dogs... On the day that the police first arrived, those giant dogs got out of the police car, with thick leather leashes tied around their necks. Some of the kids were really frightened. The kids stood perfectly still, without moving an inch. "Get the dogs out of here!" they shouted. "We don't need them here."

At first I didn't understand what they were afraid of. After all, we had dogs at the youth village, even bigger ones, and we really loved them. But Ariel immediately understood that it was the image of these dogs together with the dark uniformed policemen that frightened the kids, reminding them of the Nazi soldiers with their uniforms and their vicious German shepherd dogs. So he approached the commanding officer and quietly asked him to get rid of the dogs. Demonstrating the utmost discipline, the dogs and the accompanying policemen climbed back into the van and waited for Ariel to talk to us. "These dogs are well-trained bloodhound search dogs," Ariel explained. "They do most of the work, and without them, it will be ten times as hard to find Alex and Misha."

Yurek said, "Gang, we've got to find Alex and Misha, so let's forget about our fears. Bring on the dogs." And at the sound of the appropriate order, the dogs leaped out of the van, ready for action. We looked on in wonderment as they sniffed every inch of territory, pulling the accompanying policemen after them. For a while we hoped that it would be possible to rely on these animals. We believed that the police, the dogs, and the many volunteers would soon find Misha and Alex.

But at the end of five days, we just sat there in the

dining room, defeated and in despair. Then Yurek got up
and addressed us all. "What is this, gang? I know that
they'll come back. Alex won't give in. He has already
gone through so many things in his life. We all know
him. If they're together now, and I'm almost certain they
are, then they'll be back, you'll see."

And the next morning, like a dream that took shape
in front of our eyes, Alex and Misha appeared. Alex was
dragging Misha after him. Both of them looked very
frightened, their clothes were dirty, and they had lost a
lot of weight. They stood there, close to each other, at the
entrance of the dining room. Alex was clutching Misha's
hand, and to our astonishment, he said, "Either we'll stay
here together, or we'll die."

Ariel approached them, sat them down at the table,
and in his warm, friendly voice said, "You'll stay here,
with us, together, I promise you." So Misha stayed with
our group, despite the fact that he was younger than us.
Another folding bed was added to Alex's room, and that's
how they lived, next to each other, for months, until they
were both convinced that they would not be separated
again.

We sat there in the shower room for at least an hour,
whispering about Misha and Alex. Someone said, "It's all
because of the reparations. All this talk about the
German reparations awakens things. I also have images
running around in my head that I haven't thought of for
a long time, that I didn't want to remember."

Another girl said, "Yes, I've also been having night-mares. And Alex, he's so sensitive, he's got so many problems. Is it any wonder that it all comes back to him?" Then someone else added that it had really been quite a while since Alex and Misha last carried out their tortured moonlight ritual.

"Did you notice that this is the first time that we're talking this way, so openly, about the subject?" Yola asked.

"About what subject?" Esty wanted to know.

"About the Holocaust. When was the last time that we said the words 'Holocaust,' 'Germany,' 'reparations'?" Yola answered. And we continued to sit there, in silence, until the first light of dawn began to glimmer through the window.

"What a night," Chavi said. "It's almost tomorrow. Soon we've got to get up to go to work."

That morning, in the dining room, we acted as though nothing had happened the night before. After a night like that, Ariel always made a point of staying close to Alex, as if to protect him.

Mira, who had joined us at our vegetarians' table, asked, "Why is that counselor standing next to him like a zombie? He should say something to him."

Daniel, who was usually totally silent, responded impatiently. "Shut up already! You've been getting on my nerves since the moment you arrived here. And besides, you're not a vegetarian. So you don't even belong here at our table." His body was tensed, his fists clenched, and his eyes were closed. It was clear that it took an immense effort for him to say these things.

But Mira had skin as thick as an elephant's, and she just continued to pour out her poison. "I know some crazy people like that," she said. "In my last youth village we had two nuts who were just the same. For them the war is still going on." With that I realized that Mira had come from another youth village. I wondered where. "But they are being helped," Mira continued. "No one just leaves them like that."

Daniel cut her off, speaking very slowly, and emphasizing every word. "Don't you understand Hebrew? We don't want to hear you—enough!" And no more words were spoken until the end of the meal.

CHAPTER 4

Before each of us went off to our morning work,
Ariel said, "Gang, I want to remind everyone
who's responsible for painting the signs that they've got
to be finished. We're late. Wim and his family are arriving about five o'clock this afternoon. The heads of the
welcoming committee who are going out to the airport
have to come to the office at exactly three o'clock."

Alex reassured him, saying, "Ariel, if you mean me,
don't worry, the signs are ready. The paint just has to
dry." His voice was soft and calm, so different from last
night's wolf cries. When he spoke, a silence settled over
the dining room, as if we were all comparing the pleasant tone of his voice in the morning with the sounds
that had shattered the previous night.

Daniel was the representative from our group to the
delegation that was going to the airport to meet Wim Van
Fliman and his family upon their return from Holland.
Since I worked with Wim in the gardens, I was responsible for the flower arrangements. Daniel joined me, and

all the way from the dining room to the hothouse, we didn't exchange even a single word. But in the middle of arranging the fresh flower bouquets, Daniel suddenly said, "Do you think I exaggerated when I spoke that way to the new girl? I never spoke that way before."

"No one ever upset you that way before. And that's a good enough reason," I said.

"If she sits with us at the table tomorrow, I'll just get up and leave," he said.

"Why don't you change places with Yurek," I suggested. "He'd like that."

"Yurek's a vegetarian?" he asked.

"No, but he'll be happy." Daniel looked at me, not really understanding what I said. And I was glad to keep my sweet little secret to myself.

At five thirty, the "Dutchmen" arrived at the youth village. The van that brought Wim and his family from the airport was welcomed by all the kids from the village, who lined both sides of the path that led from the main road to the entrance. They climbed down from the van and passed under rows of colored placards painted in the blue and white colors of the Israeli flag and the blue, white, and red colors of the Dutch flag. We welcomed them with flowers and shouts of joy. And in the evening we had a party in the big hall. There were tables filled with goodies, dancing and artistic performances that were specially prepared for the occasion, and once again we remembered how the story of Wim and his family's trip to Holland began.

It was after the fall holidays. At the first Friday evening dinner after our return, Rachel, the principal, said that she had a wonderful announcement to make. "Wim Van Fliman, our very own Tuviah, our dear and beloved gardener, has had the honor of being invited by the queen of Holland, Queen Juliana, to return to Holland, the land of his birth, to receive the highest medal of honor and bravery for his courage during the days of the struggle against the Nazi conquerors." Rachel showed us the invitation, which had been sent on thick, white shining paper, with gold lining along the margins and a gold crown—the symbol of the Dutch throne—at the top of the page. The invitation was passed from hand to hand. We touched it and tried to feel the sense of something royal about it. Until that moment, our only connection with queens had been in legends and folk-tales. We were really excited; we cheered our very own Wim and sang out in a two-part harmony: "For Wim's a jolly good fellow, for Wim's a jolly good fellow, for Wim's a jolly good fellow, which nobody can deny." And then he stood up, and in his very special Hebrew, with that heavy foreign accent, he said, "But I'm not going to Holland. I've already informed Her Majesty the Queen that I'm not coming without my family. I won't travel alone. Not even to Holland. Not even to the queen."

A few days later another invitation arrived. This time it was addressed to Wim Van Fliman and family, and once again, the invitation was signed by Queen Juliana. "Mrs. Van Fliman and the children are, of course, also invited,"

it said, "and will fly together in a plane belonging to the
Dutch airlines." The timetable for the flight and the pro-
gram in Holland were listed in detail on the invitation,
and when the whole thing was read out to us, we burst
into laughter as if we all had a share in a big private joke.
We all knew that there was no and never had been a
Mrs. Wim Van Fliman and that his children were "the
Dutch group"—the seven Jewish kids who he had saved
during the war. At the end of the war, Wim had decided
that he couldn't and didn't want to be separated from
them, so when they came to Israel, he came, too.
Together with Sabin and Jacky, with Noah, Joel, Shmuel,
and with the twins, Martin and Peter. And when they
were sent to our youth village, he was right behind
them.

Wim soon converted to Judaism, and he changed his
name to Tuviah. But somehow, like many of the kids
who came to us with foreign names and were given
Hebrew names, the new name just didn't stick. We continued to call him Wim, though Rachel and the teachers
always made a point of calling him Tuviah. Wim was our
gardener, and we had the most beautiful garden in the
area. His gardens, and the seven kids, were the center of
his life. Within the village they formed a really special
group—one, big, united family. At holidays and cere-
monies they always sat next to him, and he was very
proud of them, just like a father with his kids.

We waited with tremendous anticipation to hear
their stories about Holland. After the recorder orchestra

finished playing a selection of Dutch songs, Wim and his children sat down on the stage and began to relate the fascinating story of their encounters with places they had remembered from childhood or that they had forgotten until now. They told about the emotional meeting with Wim's comrades from the underground and his medal of honor and bravery, which, resting on a blue velvet pillow, was passed from hand to hand. And then, the main thing, the highlight of the visit: They related every single detail about the ceremony in the queen's palace. We heard a description of what the queen wore, and how she spoke, and what they ate in the palace, and how the guests looked. They spoke, and we listened. We heard how everyone in the palace was astonished to discover that Wim's "children" were actually the Jewish children who he had rescued during the war, our seven friends, who immediately became great heroes in Holland.

They were interviewed on the radio, and their pictures appeared on the front page of all the most important newspapers. We passed around the Dutch newspapers, turning them page by page, feeling the newsprint. The papers were printed in a strange language, the pictures were gray and a little blurry, but we were really excited to see them. This was the first time that a picture of someone we knew had appeared in a newspaper. And in the middle of the celebration, Wim got up, pointed to a big puffed-up sack, and said, "This is it, the present for everyone at our youth village that was sent to us by my dear friends in the underground. Here, in this sack, is a lot of love and beauty from Holland. But I need help for this, so who volunteers?" We all raised our hands, without having the slightest idea what we were volunteering for.

And on the first Saturday after the return of our friends from Holland, we all climbed the hill where the domim tree stood and planted seeds and bulbs in the ground, a gift from the members of the Dutch underground. As the days passed soft delicate leaves began to blossom from the bulbs, and the seeds also began to sprout.

One day while I was standing alongside Wim at the foot of the hill, which was already covered with a carpet of green leaves, he said, "Soon, you'll see. There's going to be a miracle here. A great miracle." On that day he gave me a small delicate sapling in a clay vase, and later he transferred the sapling into a beautiful white china vessel, with a picture of a big blue windmill on its side.

"What plant is this?" I asked.

"Oh, it's a very beautiful flower," he said. "*Vergeet mij niet*—it's a flower of love."

"What does it mean?" I asked.

He said, "Ahhh, '*vergeet mij niet*' means 'don't forget me.'"

"So why don't we call it 'forget-me-not'? That sounds better in Hebrew."

"And you should know that we give this flower only to someone whom we want to remember us, so that they won't forget," said Wim.

One day as I was working in the gardens, Wim said to me, "We've got visitors. What a great honor for us. Three more beautiful flowers came to our gardens."

And I corrected him, "Not *came*, Wim, *have come*." The three "flowers" were Ayala, Chavi, and Esty, my three roommates. They asked Wim for permission to speak to me.

"Just for a few minutes, please!" they said.

I panicked. "What's wrong?" I asked.

"Don't worry, nothing happened, but we've just got to speak to you. Actually, something did happen," Ayala said, "but promise that you won't get upset."

"What happened? Tell me," I begged them.

And they began to stutter. "Well . . . your china vase . . . that beautiful one . . . from Holland, the one that Wim gave you," Esty whispered so that he wouldn't hear. "We just found it, broken. Mira did it, the monster, *she's* the one. And you also have a letter. For three days the envelope was lying on the floor under your bed. She brought the mail and didn't even bother to tell us it had arrived or to put it in the drawers. Chavi found the letters by accident, and yours was one of them. At least we saved the sapling."

I listened to them and felt my anger rising. "You don't have to talk so much," I said. "Where the hell is the letter?"

"Here, but already you're getting upset. You promised that you wouldn't," Ayala said. I looked at the envelope and immediately recognized my Aunt Alice's handwrit-

ing. I wanted to read it right away, but Ayala continued,
"We've got to do something. She's just not for us, and
maybe we're not for her. We've decided to tell Ariel that
he should take her out of our room. Don't you agree?
We'll go to him and say, 'It's either her or us.' "

Filled with impatience, I cut them off. "Before we
speak with Ariel, maybe we should speak with her," I
said.

"What is there to talk about?" Ayala asked. "We should
just tell him that we don't want her, and that's that."

Wim let me off work early, and I went back to the
room with my friends. But first I read my aunt's letter.
"Dear Aviya," she wrote, "We're leaving in two days.
We're going to Germany. To take care of our reparations.
We really didn't intend to go back there. It's a cursed
land, and I know that it will be hard for me to be there.
But still, it's about reparations, about compensation for
what they did to us. Maybe we'll be able to get some
money from them, and finally, finally, we'll be able to
manage. I hope that one day we'll come back.
Meanwhile, I'm sending you two pictures, which actually belong to you. One is of your mother and father at
their wedding. Look how beautiful they were together!
And the other is a smaller picture of your father. See how
much you look like him?" It really was a clear picture.
Among the few pictures of my father that I had managed
to steal from my mother a few years ago, there wasn't a
single picture that was so clear. I was able to make out
the lines of my father's face and look into his deep, dark

eyes. My mother once said that his eyes were big and
dark, just like mine. But only now could I see that she
was right. My father was really handsome. His name was
written on the other side of the picture, in both Hebrew
and Polish, and under the name was written the words
"Kaibeach, Haifa." Who is Kaibeach? What is Kaibeach?
What does the word mean? I didn't know. At the end of
the letter my aunt added, "When you grow up, I'll take
you to his grave. I promise."

I thought, *What does she mean "when I grow up"? What
am I now, a little girl? And why is it so hard for them to tell
me where he's buried? What are they hiding from me? I've just
got to know. It's my right. For years I've been trying to get bits
of information about my father from my mother, but she doesn't
talk, while my aunt evades. And now Aunt Alice is going away,
without even leaving an address.*

"We'll get settled a little, having a new address, and
then I'll send it to you," she wrote.

*Aunt Alice, I want to know where my father is buried. You
must tell me, now.*

When we returned to the room, Mira was sprawled
on her bed, the room was a mess, and my salvaged
sapling was resting on a small pile of earth that completely covered its exposed roots. The sapling wasn't
damaged. I filled a clay vase with some rich soil that I
brought from the hothouse, ignored Mira's presence, and
just focused on the sapling and the vase. I knew that any
word she might say would lead to an argument.
Thoughts ran through my head. Aunt Alice's letter, and

the fact that she was going to Germany, really made me
angry. *How could she?* I thought. The reparations, the
money, what was she talking about? That's exactly the
way Sarah B. spoke in the argument we had in the group,
and everyone got so mad at her.

Suddenly, Mira's voice broke through the thick
silence in the room. "It will break again, your vase. Don't
waste your time. You're all to blame. Take the bed out,
fold it up, take it out, fold it up. Everything will break
here. I'm not responsible for anything."

I couldn't control myself any longer, and I heard
myself shouting, "Who needs you here? Where does all
this evil come from? We don't want you, you hear me?
Take your things and get out of here, out of this room,
out of our lives." But Mira, of course, didn't budge. She
lay there on her bed, and I actually thought that she was
enjoying herself, as if she had expected one of us to
explode. She looked at us with her watery eyes, and a
slight smile began to appear on her lips. Chavi and Esty
were already beginning to fold their sheets on top of the
bed. *They're leaving the room*, I thought, *and I mustn't let it
happen.* "You're staying here," I said. "Let *her* leave. We're
not moving from our room." Chavi said something that
I didn't understand, and Esty answered her. This was the
first time that I had ever heard them talking to each
other in Polish.

Mira laughed maliciously and said, "I don't care if
you don't speak to me. As far as I'm concerned, you just
don't exist."

Ayala and I looked at each other. *So*, I thought, *Mira understands Polish. Is she from there too?* Actually, all we knew about her was that she came from another youth village—that was it. Since she'd arrived, she hadn't gotten a single letter. No one visited her, and no one asked about her. I thought, *Next Saturday, when we leave for vacation, she'll stay behind.* "I just don't feel like having a vacation," she had said a few days before. But maybe she had no place to go, and no one to go to.

These thoughts about Mira disturbed me. Maybe we should have behaved differently with her, tried to understand her. But the evil, there was so much evil in this one girl; I simply didn't have room in my heart for pity.

I decided that on my next Saturday vacation I would visit my mother, despite the fact that Yurek and I had arranged to take a trip to the Galilee region. That would have to wait. I'd explain it to him, and I was sure that he'd understand. I just had to find out the meaning of the words on the back of the picture of my father that I had gotten from Aunt Alice. I told myself, *I'll make my mother talk. I mustn't give in.* For years I'd been trying to make her talk, but she always withdrew into her illness. Mother suffered from serious emotional problems. She was very sick. And one mustn't make her angry. I always treat her gently, but this time, I just had to know. Who is Kaibeach? Or what is Kaibeach? Who was my father—really? How did he die, and where is he buried? I thought, *I've got to know now!*

★   ★   ★

On Friday afternoon the village began to empty out. We left for a "traveling vacation," a vacation that would last until Saturday evening.

I was almost the last one to leave. Yurek kept pushing me to hurry up; after all, it was Friday, and I might miss the last bus. I kept on dawdling, stealing a few more moments with him. Yurek accompanied me to the main road, and afterward he turned to take the path back to the youth village. His image, drifting into the distance, became smaller and smaller. I could still make out his golden curls waving in the wind, until he completely disappeared from sight. He would spend the Sabbath at the youth village, together with the other "abandoned ones." The homeless. This thought really made me sad. I shouldn't have left him there alone. But the urgent need to see my mother pushed those thoughts away.

CHAPTER 5

I stood on the main road, alone, looking at the rain that was approaching from afar. I watched the heavy black clouds that covered the horizon. *I hope it won't rain, not now,* I thought. *After all, there's no shelter here, and I'll be totally exposed.*

My prayer was answered. A small black car stopped alongside me. The driver, an old man with a pleasant face, asked, "Where are you going?" When he heard that I was going to Petach Tikva, he said, "You're in luck. I'll take you there even before the sun sets and the Sabbath begins. Are you from Petach Tikva?" he asked. "Who are your parents?" he wanted to know. And I, in order to avoid any unnecessary conversation, said the name of Yurek's family. When the man said that he didn't know us, I answered that we just moved in last week. "Petach Tikva is a wonderful town," he said. "All you need is health and a good job. I'm sure you'll be happy there. Don't worry, I'll bring you right to the center of town." I hoped that this was a good start to the beginning of a

good vacation. I so wanted my vacation with Mother to
be a happy one. I was always a little nervous when I went
to see my mother. I was never sure what state she would
be in. It started to rain. The windshield wiper dancing
along the front window with a steady beat had a hyp-
notic effect on me. I was in a trance. The driver was
finishing those familiar opening words. (These drivers
really make me laugh: They're all equipped with the
same opening sentences, they all have the same questions.) "Why do you hitchhike? Where are you from?
What is a young girl like you doing alone on the road at
such a late hour?"

Whenever drivers asked me these questions, I always
answered, "I'm used to hitchhiking. It's cheaper and
faster than buses that stop at all the stations. And until
now I've only had good experiences, so I don't feel as if
I'm taking any risks." In most instances that last sentence
was the end of the conversation. And then there was
silence. I was waiting for the moment, trying to guess if
the driver would try to begin a longer conversation. But
this driver was silent, concentrating entirely on the road.

Heavy rain began to fall, the window began to fog
up, and it became difficult to see. Every so often the driver opened the side window so that fresh air would
come in and the fog would evaporate. The cold, stinging
air was refreshing. The car moved ahead, and I drifted
into imaginary conversations with my mother. My
father's picture was hidden in my bra under my clothes,
like a good luck charm held close to my body. From

time to time I ran my hand over it, felt the small rectangle lying close to my heart. *I'll pull the picture out,* I thought to myself. *I'll put it on the palm of my hand, and I'll present it to my mother. As close as possible, but not too close to her face. I'll wait for her reaction, and as usual, she'll ignore everything. But this time I won't give in, and I'll tell her, "This is my father, isn't it? You know that it's him. Say something."* And she, after a long silence, would ask me to turn off the light *"because we're not rich, like the Rothschilds..."* Or she'd ask if I was cold and whether I had already eaten. *"You've got to eat,"* she would of course tell me. *"Aviya, you're a growing girl."* But I would insist, *"No, Mother. Don't change the subject. Not this time. I came so that you would talk to me. So that you would tell me who I am, who my father is. It's my right to know! I'm a big girl already, and I don't know anything about my father."* She would turn her back on me, and I would turn her around and not let her get away with evading me. She'd get angry and say, *"I've got a headache. I don't feel well."* Then she'd ask for her medicine. *I'd hold the medicine, shake the pills so that she'd hear them rattling in the jar, but I wouldn't give them to her until she spoke.*

Actually, I knew that I wouldn't behave that way. *It was dangerous. Mother had to have her medicine the moment she asked for it. But I'll look into her eyes and I won't let her get away with it. I mustn't let my eyes drop. I've got to trap her, and I can't let her break. She'll be forced to explain who Kaibeach is. What Kaibeach is. And she will ask, "Where did you get this picture?" And I'll say, "From Alice. Aunt Alice sent it to me two days before she left for Germany. Did you know that she was going? She went back there, Mother. She went to get money from the Germans." And Mother would be silent, and I'd continue, "Before she left, she sent father's picture to me and wrote that it belongs to me. And now, Mother, there's no one else to tell me about him. Just you. My friends at the youth village are orphans, but at least they know who their parents were. They remember the faces of their mothers and fathers, but all I have is a black hole. I can't stand it anymore!" At that Mother might explode, and that was forbidden. Her outbursts were dangerous. I heard her screaming in her high, frightening voice and saw her face fall and grow ugly, right before my eyes. I was scared.*

Then the driver asked, "Young lady, don't you feel well?" He pulled over to the side of the road. The car stopped, and I really panicked. What does he want? Why did he stop so suddenly?

As if I were waking from a bad dream, I asked him anxiously, "Why did you stop, Mister? Why?"

And he quietly responded, "It seemed as if something had happened to you. I spoke to you and you didn't answer me."

"I'm okay," I mumbled. "I'm fine."

The driver got out of the car for a moment, despite the fact that it was still raining. He brought a blue thermos back from the trunk and poured me some tea in a plastic cup. I drank, and so did he. "You're not dressed warmly enough," he said. "You've got to take care in this weather. Maybe you're catching the flu. When you get home, get into bed with some tea and lemon and a warm blanket. It will pass." The good driver drove me to the center of town, and I ran home, to Mother.

I was still running, and suddenly, I realized that I was lost. I just couldn't remember which way to turn, how to get home. It was a new neighborhood. Mother had moved there just a few months earlier, and I had been there only once. I was so happy for her. She finally had a stone house, in a new neighborhood, with different people. I hated the old neighborhood. It was filled with bad people, and bad people have bad kids. I so hoped that she would be happy in the new neighborhood, that the old illness wouldn't return, that they wouldn't hear her scream, that they wouldn't take her away. I kept looking for the way to Mother's new home, and only when I came upon the red police station did I realize that I was on the right road. I thought, *From the police station, I turn right, and then left, and it's the third house from the corner.*

Mother was busy when I came in; she had a visitor. When I realized who it was, I panicked, and even forgot to hug her. Sitting next to the table was dumb Avramel, crazy Avramel. Avramel cast his shadow over the town, particularly over the girls. People said that he was a threat to little girls. They said that he had been seen taking down his pants in public and exposing himself. He wandered around the streets of the town, and everyone ran away from him. And here he was, sitting next to my mother. When he saw me, Avramel got up and growled. His voice was really frightening. When he opened his

almost toothless mouth, Mother jumped in, "You know
Avramel, yes? Don't be afraid."

I whispered to Mother behind his back, "He's dangerous, Mother. He's crazy."

And Mother, who knew that the dumb one was also
deaf, said aloud, "Even someone who's crazy needs a roof
over his head and some bread to eat." She didn't get up
until he finished his meal. Afterward she gave him a sack
of oranges and biscuits, and spoke to him very slowly,
with great patience, making very large movements with
her lips so he could understand. In order to make things
easier for him, she also made signs with her hands.
"You'll come again, won't you, Avramel?" He nodded
his head yes and once again growled like an animal. He
smiled, and her face glowed, and then he puckered his
lips, as if he were sending her kisses. Mother laughed and
said in Yiddish, "*Gei shoin, Avramel, as komet shoin dar
Shabbas,*" which means "Go already, Avramel, the Sabbath
is coming." With that, Avramel left. Mother gathered up
his dishes, saying, "He needs pity. In this rain, in the
streets, alone, all the time. You know, he's got a house, and
a rich father who doesn't want to have anything to do
with him. Can you imagine that? Isn't that father
ashamed of himself?"

I felt the picture that was close to my heart, looked
into my mother's eyes, and decided: *This is the moment.*
She's in a good mood now. I said, "Mother, come sit
down for a while. I'd also like some tea and biscuits." I sat
down next to the table. The seat of Avramel's chair was

still warm. Mother prepared some tea, we both drank, and afterward I asked her, "Mother, what is Kaibeach? Who is it?" Mother stared at me, her beautiful eyes opened even wider than usual. She just kept staring at me, her eyes not moving, not saying a single word. "Mother, this is why I came to see you." I took out father's picture and cradled it in the palm of my hand, as if it were a precious treasure. I showed it to her very carefully, not too close, but close enough for her to clearly see it without touching it. That's exactly how I had imagined this moment when riding in the car. "That's my father, isn't it?" Mother looked at me and didn't say a word. "Speak to me, Mother," I demanded. "I've got to know—you've got to tell me about him." I stood very close to her, hoping that I'd manage to make her say something. But she continued her silence, so I turned toward her sewing machine, where she kept a little notebook with a pencil attached to it on a string. "Write," I said. "If it's hard for you to talk, write something. Just a few words, Mother."

But she remained silent, not a single muscle moving on her face.

Finally she said, "You'll catch cold that way. Your clothes are too thin."

I stood right next to her and shouted, "I'm okay, Mother. I'm warm enough. I asked you something; answer me. I won't give up, Mother, do you hear? I'm going crazy. I just can't stand it any longer. I've got to know who I am, who my father was, where his grave is."

This was the first time that I had ever raised my voice to my mother, that I was ever rude to her. I simply ignored what was usually forbidden to me. I knew that Mother was very sensitive. Mother had had a hard life, which was the cause of her emotional problems. Suddenly, she got up from the table and went over to the big open sacks that were standing under the windowsill. She'd gathered these sacks from the grocery store and the market place. They used to hold sugar and flower. Now Mother filled them with old clothes, tools, sheets, and dishes to give to the needy, the elderly, the orphans, and the poor. She worried about everybody. She used to walk through the streets of the town, dragging the sacks behind her. The children used to run after her, mocking her loudly. "There goes Henia with her rags, there goes the old clothes lady…" they'd say. And she, as usual, would cover her ears, wouldn't listen, wouldn't see. The main thing was to decide what to put in the sacks and how to divide it among the needy. And when the sacks were empty, she'd wash and dry them and put them back in their place under the windowsill. Then she'd start collecting all over again. Now she went over to the sacks and started pressing their contents with her hands.

I begged her, "Speak to me, Mother. You've got to. Someone's got to speak to me."

She looked at me with her big, wide-open eyes and said, "Don't you see that we've got to tie the sacks? You're standing and talking at the very moment that I need another pair of hands." And she was already bend-ing down to gather up the rope that was lying on the ground, ready to tie the sacks. I pushed her into an upright position, threw away the rope, and kicked the sack.

"You should be ashamed of yourself," she shouted. "It took me so long to collect these things. Poor miserable people are waiting for the wonderful things that are in these sacks. And you, you don't care, you just think about yourself. You're so selfish."

"Mother," I said, "I'm going. I'm leaving you. You can ask dumb Avramel to help you with the sacks and with your needy people. You're not going to see me here anymore, Mother."

She sat down next to the table, and for a moment I thought that, despite everything, I had succeeded; she was finally ready to talk. But then she said, "Close the windows so that the neighbors won't hear how rude you are to your mother. No one should know what goes on in our house."

I pleaded, I spoke quietly, to make sure that she would stay calm and that no one would hear. "Mother, that's all I'm asking you. Speak to me, and I'll never bother you about it again. I swear." She just sat there, with her hands folded on the table, and looked through me as if I weren't there. Once again that familiar frightening look had returned to her eyes, and from that moment on, I knew it made no difference whether I was right next to her or not. To her, I just wasn't there. She sank into her own private world, a world that I could

never enter. And as usual, I knew exactly what to do and
how to do it. I knew where her medicine was, what and
how much to give her whenever this happened. So I ran
to the kitchen, found the medicine, put the jar of pills
and bottle of drops together with a full cup of water on
the table. I waited for a moment and almost bent down
to hug her, but instead, I grabbed my knapsack that was
still lying next to the table. I left the house and just ran,
without knowing where.

I really surprised myself, leaving my mother that way.
I hoped that she would come after me, that she'd try to
stop me, that she'd call my name, that she'd beg me to
come back, that she'd promise that she'd speak to me. I
waited, but I didn't hear her voice.

Turning toward the house, I saw her hands closing
the blinds. I continued on my way. The streets were
empty, and the stores were shut. The Sabbath was in the
air. I headed toward the main road and waited for a ride.
It was already dark by the time I reached the edge of
town. I stood there alone. Only a few cars went by, and
their drivers simply ignored my outstretched hand.
Night fell. It was cold, and I was a little frightened. I kept
shifting my weight from foot to foot, rubbing my hands
together, and blowing into my cupped palms. Tears covered my face.

I waited for at least an hour and began to fear that I
might have to return to my mother, to knock on her
door, and to ask her forgiveness so that she would give
me shelter for the night. "Please, I don't want to have to

do that," I said silently to myself. That's when a car
stopped.

A young man and woman were sitting in the front
seat, and behind them, in the back seat, were a girl about
my age and a little boy. I squeezed in between them and
nestled up against their warm woolen coats. The girl said,
"Wow, Mother, look at her braid." She pulled my braid
and passed it forward, close to her mother's face, as if it
were hers.

Her mother turned around and said, "It really is
beautiful. It must take your mother a long time to comb
it every morning. Don't worry, Nili, you'll have one too,
just like that. You can trust your mother." I looked at the
girl's frizzy hair and thought that she would never ever
have a braid like mine.

"It's a little crowded in here, but that's better than
standing for another hour on the road," said the woman.
She warned her daughter, "Don't you ever dare travel by
hitchhiking, Nili." And to me she said, "You're really
lucky that we stopped, because it could be very dangerous out here." Then she asked me if I needed any money.
"What's the problem? Do you need a few coins for the
bus? I can give them to you." I answered that I was used
to traveling this way, that most of my friends travel by
hitchhiking. She mumbled, "Well, it used to be safe. But
not anymore. You know, all sorts of suspicious types wander around the roads, and God knows where they come
from." I didn't say anything else and hoped that would be
the end of the conversation.

Her husband, who had been silent until then, said,
"Stop frightening the girl. Enough." They started talking
about members of their family and almost forgot about
me.

When we neared the path that leads from the main
road to the youth village, I asked the driver to stop. "This
is where I get off," I said.

"But there's nothing here," objected the woman.
When I explained that my youth village was at the end
of the path, the woman said, "Are you from an orphan-
age? Are you an orphan?" I smiled and didn't answer.
"Under no circumstances. You're not getting off here. We
won't let you walk all alone down this long path," said
the woman. The car turned toward the youth village, and
when we passed by the hill, I asked the driver to slow
down, so I could see if Yurek was there. At this late hour
the domim tree was his alone. I hoped that he would be
there. "It's so dark here, it's frightening. What's that
mountain on the right?" asked the woman.

"It's a hill," I responded, "and at the edge of the hill,
up there—" I pointed to the shadow of the tree, which
stood out like a bouquet of feathers on a giant hat—"is
a wonderful tree. A domim tree. It might look a little
frightening now, but during the day, it's really beautiful
here."

Musa, the guard, rode toward us on his horse as we
stopped at the gates of the youth village. "This is my
ride," I said to Musa.

The woman scolded him, "Mister, if I may be permitted to say so, I don't think it's right that you let your orphans wander around on the roads like this at night. It's dangerous. You should have pity on these kids."

Musa was a little embarrassed as he looked at me. "The lady is right. I'll report this to the principal." Then he winked at me.

I thanked them and suggested, "If you'd like to visit here, just ask for me, the longest braid in the Sunflower group."

CHAPTER 6

They left, and Musa offered me a ride to my group's quarters. I climbed on, and as we trotted into the village, I held onto his powerful back, while Horsey, Musa's giant dog, plodded along behind us. "Are you from Sunflower?" he suddenly asked. "Yes," I said, "from Ariel's group."

"Well, there's a big celebration going on. Don't you know that a great miracle happened in your group?"

"What miracle?" I asked.

"They found the father of one of your girls, alive, in Poland. A tremendous celebration has been going on since the afternoon."

"Who is it? What's her name?" I asked.

"I don't know," he answered, "but she's from Sunflower."

"Take me there," I urged him. "I don't believe you."

The lights were on in our group's quarters, and I could see that everyone was huddled together. I saw Yurek standing next to Sarah B., and I trembled. *He's gone back to her,* I thought. *They're together again, like always. As if nothing had changed.* I tried to call him, but my voice cracked. I tried again. "Yurek!" He turned, but couldn't recognize me in the dark.

Musa called to him, "Here, Yurek. She's here." And he ran toward me, extended his hands and helped me off the horse. This was the first time that I felt his body so close to mine. We stood there together for a moment, and he didn't ask why I had returned or what had happened at Mother's house. We just stood there quietly, and it was warm and good.

Afterward he put his hand in mine and said, "It's a great day; wonderful things are happening here."

Yola was sitting on her bed in Room 4, leaning against the wall, holding on to Lalka, her little pillow. She never went to sleep without it. That pillow was once pink, and maybe even beautiful, but now it looked like a faded rag. Even when we went out on hikes, she'd stuff the poor pillow into her knapsack and would take it out at night before we went to sleep. Sometimes we were pretty mean, hiding Lalka somewhere. Yola would really get angry and threaten that she wouldn't go back to her room until we returned the pillow. Last time, when we returned the pillow, she attached a long, winding ribbon to it and tied one end to the foot of the bed. Ever since, Lalka has been attached to her like a dog on a leash.

Now she sat there on her bed with her pillow, while the ribbon wound between her hands and legs like a long snake. A little tray was next to her bed, holding a glass of water and a wet towel. Every so often she would drink some water, and Ruth, the nurse, who was standing next to her, would encourage her, "Drink, Yola, it's good for you. You should drink a lot."

All the kids who hadn't gone on vacation were clustered together at the entrance to the room. They'd been standing like that since the afternoon, staring at Yola in wonder, and I realized that I didn't even have to ask what happened and how it became known. They knew the whole story. Sarah B. was standing there, next to handsome Avner Engel from the twelfth grade, and she seemed to be presiding over the whole affair. "Gang, move away a little from the door, let some air in. She needs air," she said, and gently pushed some of the others away. When she saw me next to Yurek, Sarah B. grabbed Avner's hand, as if to make sure that we knew that she wasn't alone. All the girls at the village were interested in Avner Engel because he was a handsome sabra—native Israeli—and very talented. Now he was hers. Sarah B. made an effort to be friendly. "Come," she said to me, "go say hello to Yola. It will make her happy." She acted as though she was the head of a reception committee. I went in and hugged Yola, and even before I had a chance to ask Yola how she found out, the words came tumbling forth as if she had rehearsed them over and over again.

"I was about to leave for the Sabbath," she said, "to visit my aunt in Ra'anana, when suddenly they called me to the office. I thought it was a telephone call, or maybe a letter. And then I saw Ruthie the nurse standing next to Rachel and Ariel. They said 'Come in and sit down.' So I sat down. And then Rachel hugged me and said, 'Yola, my dear, a wonderful miracle has happened. You're no longer an orphan; you've got a father. Your father is alive!' So there I was, sitting there, still not understanding what they were talking about. Rachel continued to explain that I have a father and he's alive and living in Poland. They found in him Warsaw. All those years he was looking for me, and now, thank God, he's been found. And then I fainted. I can't remember anything. Afterward they brought me to the room, and Ruthie's been taking care of me ever since. Can you believe it? It's hard to believe, no?"

Ruth broke in, "Yola darling, take it easy. You're getting excited again." And she moved the glass of water close to Yola's lips. After Yola took a sip, Ruth put the wet towel on her forehead, and picking up the medicine bottle, she asked, "Do you want another pill, Yola?" Yola said no.

Ruth continued to sit next to Yola on the bed. She held Yola's hand and coaxed her, "Yola, maybe you'll rest a little now? You've been talking constantly, without a stop."

But Yola kept on mumbling, "My father's alive. Can you believe it? My father's alive."

Mira, who was standing with the bunch of kids clustered at the entrance, muttered, "Well, what can you

expect? We've heard this all before. Can't she say anything else?"

Sarah B. heard her and turned on her. "You're disgusting, Mira. Get out of here!" Mira turned to leave, and
no one reacted to the curse that she tossed behind her.

That night I slept in Yola's room. "It wouldn't be
good for her to be alone on a night like this," said Ruth.
"Someone's got to stay with her." I immediately volunteered. I preferred to sleep in Yola's room, on Sarah A.'s
bed, and not in my own bed, together in the same room
with Mira.

Yola didn't sleep a wink the whole night. She just sat
there and talked about her father. She told me what he
looked like—a young man, with black curly hair, with
thin-rimmed glasses on his nose, and large, bright eyes.
"He had eyes like flashlights," she said, "and above his
right eyebrow he had a little scar, a souvenir from a fight
with a bunch of Polish ruffians when he was a kid." And
then she said, "I also remember my mother, as if we parted only yesterday. I remember every detail of her face."
Yola's long eyelashes rested on her cheeks, and she added,
"She died in Auschwitz, that's what my aunt told me. She
was with her at the concentration camp." Yola was quiet,
and then she let out a long, heavy sigh and started to
leave the room.

"Where are you going, Yola?" I asked.

"To the bathroom."

When she came back, her eyes were even redder.
"Don't be ashamed to cry in front of me, Yola," I said.

She wiped her nose. "I'm not crying. You know I'm not like that. Have you ever seen me cry? It's only my eyes, they're always irritating me."

Fatigue almost overwhelmed her, but she continued to struggle against it, wet her face with the moist towel, and kept on talking. Every so often she'd remember more details, and she'd tell me a few more stories. "Once he picked me up in the air. Maybe I was about three years old, and he dropped me. He was horrified and ran away from home. My mother had shouted, 'The girl, the girl!' I can still remember her scream. Sometimes at night, I can hear her screaming, though I want to remember other things, happier things. Why do I remember that scream?"

I let her talk, and I envied the memories that she carried with her all these years. "I would give anything to be able to see my father's face, even once," I said. Yola didn't seem to hear me. "I also remember his hand, so strong, so big, as it held my little hand. He had a strong hand, a real *lappa*." That Polish word *lappa* really made me laugh.

I said, "Soon, Yola, soon you'll be holding his *lappa* in yours again." We both laughed and laughed. Her face was streaked with tears, and she was laughing and crying at the same time. I laughed and cried with her. As I was running out of breath, I said, "Enough, Yola. You've got to sleep a little. It's almost morning. You need strength for tomorrow."

Suddenly she straightened up and asked, "Do you remember your father?"

"No," I said. "I never saw him. He died a long time ago. Before I was born."

"Maybe it's better that way, to be an orphan from the start. Sometimes memories can kill," Yola said.

Finally Yola's fatigue overcame her. She stopped talking, her head fell backward, and her eyes closed. I helped her into her bed, with her clothes still on and with Lalka held tightly in her hands. I pulled the pillow under her head and covered her with a blanket. Her face looked calm, like a baby's. It was already morning, and the room was flooded with light. I closed the curtains and darkened the room, so that she wouldn't be disturbed. It looked like she was sleeping peacefully. For a whole hour, I sat next to her, not closing an eye. Since she couldn't see me, I let myself look at her closely and tried to guess what she was seeing, in her dreams, now that she was alone with herself. All at once, her breathing became heavy, and her face, which had been so calm, became distorted with pain. She tossed and turned in her sleep as if she were struggling with somebody or something who was hurting her and not letting go.

I whispered, "Yola," and lightly touched her arm, but she didn't wake up. She kept uttering unclear words and syllables. I tried to understand what she was saying but didn't succeed. "Yola," I whispered again, "what's wrong, Yola?" I rested my hand on her forehead, and her face grew calm. Slowly, slowly, her whole body seemed to relax. She grabbed my hand, which was close to her, and held on to it like a baby wrapping its hand around the

finger of an adult. I was afraid to move, because I didn't
want to wake her. My body was frozen like a rock, my
head was getting heavy, and I just wanted to sleep, but I
couldn't break away from her grasp.

I don't know how long I stood that way, with my
hand in hers. Eventually, Sarah B. found me. She came
into the room right after breakfast and released me from
Yola's grasp.

For a moment I didn't understand why my hand felt
as solid as lead, what I was doing in a room that wasn't
mine, and why my body hurt and my head felt so heavy.
Only when Sarah B. began to organize the room to get
it ready for the new day did the previous night's experiences come back to me. "The gang will start coming
here any minute now, and we have to make sure that
they don't wake her up," she whispered, leading me
toward the door. "Rest a little; I'll take care of everything," she said. I knew that I could rely on her, on Sarah
B., and I tiptoed out of the room.

When I got to my room, Mira was still sleeping. I
looked at her. She was curled up into herself, with only
her face peeking out of the blanket. There wasn't even a
hint of the malice that usually showed in her face. I knelt
down on my knees near my bed and reached under the
mattress to look for my diary. To my surprise, it wasn't in
its regular place. Before I left to visit my mother, I
checked to make sure it was in its place, waiting for me
until I got back. As always, I was afraid to take my diary
with me on my visits to my mother's house, since she

might discover it. I lifted the mattress and found the
diary lying at the other end of the bed. I immediately
knew that someone had touched it. Only Mira could
have been nosy enough to do it. I had no doubt that it
was her. I turned toward her, boiling with anger. I wanted to wake her up, but her eyes were already open. She
was sitting on her bed. "Why did you do it?" I asked.
"Why? There are rules, don't you understand? No one
sneaks a look. No one reads another girl's diary. Aren't
you ashamed?" She was silent, and glared at me as if she
were preparing for a fight. I shook the diary in her face,
and all of the dried flowers that had been hidden among
its pages fell and spread around the floor. I bent down to
pick them up. There was something ridiculous about this
kneeling on all fours. I looked like a dog on the floor,
and she laughed. I got up, holding the dried flowers in
my hand. I crushed them, and spread the powder they
made on her bed.

"Look at how you look because of a few dried flowers and leaves," she sneered.

"I don't care how I look," I sneered back. Mira sat on
her bed, shook the flower dust to the floor and was
silent. "Did you also read the other diaries?" I asked. Her
face was frozen. "Make sure that you put them back in
their places," I said, "so the girls won't know what you
did. I won't tell, you can count on that."

She just looked at me, and after a minute, she said,
"Aren't you wasting time? You should run to complain
under your stupid domim tree; he's waiting for you." I

almost hit her, but I didn't have the strength. I felt humil-
iated and exposed. *She knows everything,* I thought. *And I
don't know anything about her.* I felt terribly insulted and
ran to the bathroom.

Instead of kneeling on the floor to write, I raised the
toilet seat, opened the thick diary, and began to tear out
page after page. I tore the pages into smaller and smaller
pieces. The paper turned into crumbs of words. My
secrets, thoughts, fears, and joys—everything fell apart,
and I threw it all into the toilet. The fragments of my
diary were flushed away in the rushing flow of the water.
All that was left was the hard cover. I trampled on it with
my feet, broke whatever was left of it, and tossed it into
the garbage.

Afterward, I splashed my face with cool water, looked
in the mirror, and said to myself, "Just don't regret it
now." I knew that my diary, which had been my closest
friend, was gone. I was alone in the shower room and
could cry over it without being seen. I wet my long hair
and felt that I was fresh and clean. I said to myself,
"Now, that's over. It's time to look ahead. I'm a big girl
now; let's see how I can get along without my diary."

On my way back to the room, I saw Yurek standing
in front of the door holding some sandwiches. "Here's
your breakfast," he said. As usual, he had stretched out his
hand to me before he had begun to talk. And I, confused
at such a moment, wanted to say that there was no need
to shake hands every time we met, but I didn't dare say
that to him. So I offered a limp hand. "Make it stronger,"

he said. "I want to feel your hand."

He asked about Yola. He wanted to know how and when she fell asleep. I told him, but I didn't say a word to him about Mira and my diary. We started to walk toward the hill. Our legs began to lead us there almost automatically. We simply met and began walking toward our regular place, to our domim tree. I heard Zevick call after us, "Wait a minute." We stopped. He came close to us and said, "Take me with you. Do you mind if I come with you?" The three of us went up the hill and sat there at the foot of the tree, looking around at the green fields and the distant villages that were spread out in front of us. We listened to the silence, and we knew: In a few hours, everyone would come back from their Sabbath vacation and that would be the end of the silence.

Suddenly, Zevick said, as if he were speaking to himself, "It's a coincidence, just a coincidence, that this miracle happened to Yola. It can't happen again, can it?" Yurek rested his hand on Zevick's shoulder and didn't say a word. Zevick reached out his hand to me, and I held it, and Yurek reached out his other hand and held mine. We sat there together, with arms entwined, really close to one another. Zevick bowed his head. I couldn't see his face, just his tears that began to fall and moisten the ground.

The rumor about Yola's miracle began to spread. The moment the kids returned from their Sabbath vacation, they all made their way toward our group's quarters. Yola

told her story once again, and each kid who repeated the
story added new details, in accordance with a very fertile
imagination. Within one day, Yola's father became a very
important figure in the Polish government, and someone
even knew that he had been found in the middle of a
thick forest, in a cave that had been carved out during
the war, and all these years he had been hiding in the terrible forest.

That same evening, Saturday night after the Sabbath,
Rachel, the principal, gathered all of us together into the
big hall. She said, "Dear pupils, the family of children at
the youth village Udim, we've gathered here today to
celebrate with our friend Yola Mintz from the Sunflower
group the wonderful miracle that has happened to her.
And I must tell you, this is really a rare occurrence." She
emphasized these words to make sure that we didn't
delude ourselves into thinking that this sort of event
would begin to happen on a regular basis. "Yola's father
was found living in Poland, in the city of Warsaw. And
we are making every effort to arrange a meeting
between them. Different bodies are involved in this
effort, both in Israel and abroad. If things work out, in
the next few days, Yola will leave for Poland and will
meet her father. We all congratulate you, Yola, this big
family of children and teachers at Udim, and we are all
glad about your happiness." Rachel finished her comments, and silence reigned in the hall. Then a
tremendous round of applause spread through the room.

Avner Engel from the twelfth grade got up on the

stage with his accordion and began to play a familiar folk tune.

We were supposed to dance, but the kids just stood there, staring at Yola. There were those who dared to move close to where she sat, and who looked and whispered. It was hard to make out what they were saying, but it was clear that, overnight, Yola had become a heroine of our village. And when we finally got up in order to leave the hall, Sarah B. once again activated her talents and cleared the way for Yola. Of course, she couldn't resist passing first alongside the stage and signaling with her hands to Avner Engel, who responded by coming toward her and leaning in her direction. Thus, the entire village saw, at that very moment, the intimate connection between Sarah B. and handsome Avner Engel.

She whispered something to him that none of us could hear. He nodded his head yes, she waved good-bye to him, and he responded with a wink. The language of lovers. A familiar language that aroused our envy. After she finished this performance before the entire village, Sarah B. was free to carry out her big role. Yola was hers, and now she had to get her out of the hall. "Make way," she directed. "What are you all looking at?" She grabbed Yola's hand and led her out, and when a girl from another group came over and asked to give something to Yola, Sarah B. said that Yola shouldn't be disturbed. Sarah B. told the girl to leave whatever it was near the living quarters of the Sunflower group. With that, the girl simply ran out of the hall.

CHAPTER 7

Whe we got back to the group's quarters, on the doorstep of Yola's room, lying under a big rock, we found a makeshift envelope constructed of folded notebook paper. "To Yola of the Sunflower group," was written on the envelope, and inside, we found a note: "Yola, when you'll be there, in Poland, look for this man for me. He's my father." The name of a man was written there in Polish. In big, clear letters. And that was only the beginning. During the next few days we kept finding a lot of little envelopes and notes, all addressed to Yola, and all with a request: "When you're in Poland, could you please look for this man. This woman. My father. My mother. My brother. My sister. Look for them for me."

Sarah B., who turned out to be a really good organizer, made a little box out of a cardboard carton, covered it with white paper, drew a big blue arrow on it, and wrote in big red letters: REQUESTS FOR YOLA MINTZ IN CONNECTION WITH HER TRIP TO POLAND, PLACE HERE.

PLEASE DON'T DISTURB. And at the bottom, she added
the words THANK YOU. She hung the improvised box on
a nail in the wall, to the right of the entrance to Room
4, Yola's room. And that way, the box filled up, without
disturbing Yola's much-needed rest.

A few days passed, and a package arrived for Yola from
her father in Poland. As soon as Yola opened the box, and
the thick paper that covered it fell to the floor, Chavi
grabbed the wrapping paper and tore off the Polish
stamps. There were six big stamps, covered with black
postmarks. We were dying of curiosity, waiting to know
what was in the package, when Sarah B. ordered in her
commanding voice, "Chavi, enough. We want to see
what's inside." And when Yola opened the package, there
was a letter written by her father in Polish.

"I hardly remember any Polish," said Yola.

In the package there was also a dress. A fine, white
muslin dress, with pink dots and little flowers embroidered with bright pink thread near the neck. It was a tiny
dress. And when Yola spread it out on her bed, it looked
even smaller. We stood around the bed, amazed by the
appearance of this wonder, feeling the wrapping paper
that covered the package. Then we touched the little
dress and turned it inside out. I saw my friends bringing
it close to their faces, smelling the cloth, maybe sensing
the fragrances of there.

Mira suddenly appeared, without anyone having
called her. We heard her saying, "Why did he send you

such a small dress? Doesn't he know how old you are?"
Sarah B. pinched Mira on the arm to shut her up, to tell
her not to hurt Yola's feelings. But Mira wouldn't give
up; she even struck Sarah B. on the hand. Sarah B. held
back, not wanting to start a fight. The dress amazed
everyone, except Mira.

"Maybe that's the way he remembers you. Little like
that," someone suggested.

"No, no," Yola said, with some confusion. "It isn't for
me at all, this dress. Now I understand. When I was little
I had a doll exactly this size. He must have sent the dress
for my doll. He wanted to make me laugh, my father."

Sarah B., who was presiding over the entire occasion,
cut the discussion off by declaring, "Girls, we have to
prepare for the trip. We have to get Yola ready so that she
can travel to Poland in style. The announcement about
the trip will surely arrive in the next few days, so we all
have to embroider her a nice blouse before she goes."

"No. Not one blouse," Ayala said, "two blouses. We'll
embroider a white blouse for the trip. She'll be wearing
it when she gets off the plane. I suggest that we embroider the white blouse with red and blue thread. She can
wear it with an A-line skirt, in workers' blue. There's a
huge role of that cloth in the storehouse. And we'll also
prepare a black embroidered blouse. A Sabbath blouse,
for going out. Maybe he'll want to take her to a coffee
house or a concert. It will be very nice to go out with a
black embroidered blouse."

We were really carried away, very excited, and even

forgot to ask Yola's opinion. She just stood there, next to
us in the room, and we spoke about her as if she weren't
there. Ayala's suggestion was immediately accepted, and
we divided up the tasks among the girls. Chavi and Esty
went to take her measurements. The next morning we
would cut the cloth in the handicrafts room, we'd sew,
and begin to embroider. Each of us would have to con-
tribute a row or two of embroidery. We were all very
excited. Ayala suggested that we weave a Tiberias belt, a
belt woven with shades of red that was very fashionable.

We began to prepare Yola for her trip to Poland, to
her father. We treated her like a bride getting ready for
her wedding. Every day after class we embroidered and
sewed. The blouses moved from hand to hand, and each
new row got us more and more excited. When my turn
came to add a row, I tried to get out of it. "I've got two
left hands," I said. "I'll just ruin the beautiful blouse."

But the girls encouraged me. "We won't let you get
away with it," they said. "Everyone has to embroider."

Ayala stood next to me while I embroidered, and she
helped me. "It's beautiful," she said. "Stop trying to con-
vince yourself that you're not talented. Look how
everyone really likes it." I passed the blouse on to Chavi,
and she passed it on to Esty.

"And what about me?" asked Mira. We were all very
surprised to hear this, since we hadn't spoken to Mira for
days.

"Do you want to embroider?" Ayala said. Mira didn't
answer, but just took the blouse and embroidered a real-

ly pretty row. Without saying anything, she added another one. After she finished, she left the blouse on her bed
for us to pass on.

When the blouses were almost ready, we took Yola to
the shower room. "Try them on," we said. "Try the
blouses and the skirt. Let's see how you look in your new
clothes."

Yola hesitated for a second. "Maybe I shouldn't. They
look wonderful, really. But it's better that I not wear
them until the trip."

We insisted. "Why not, Yola? We just want to see how
you look in the clothes, how you'll look when he meets
you."

But Yola wouldn't give in. "My aunt from Ra'anana
says it's forbidden, that we Jews have a custom, that we
don't buy diapers until the baby is born," she explained.

We brought the clothes back to her room and spread
them out on her bed: The blue skirt with its rich, flow-
ing bottom covered the entire width of the bed; we
tucked the white blouse inside it, with the beautiful red
Tiberias belt in between them, which had been woven
by Ayala in record time. We stood there in awe, looking
at the beautiful clothes that we had made with our own
hands.

Chavi abruptly approached the clothes, picked them
up from the bed, and brought them close to her body,
tightening the skirt and the blouse, as if she were alone
in the room. We watched her movements in total silence.
Suddenly, she burst into tears, put the clothes back on

the bed, and ran out of the room. I immediately followed
her, but she ran so fast that I couldn't keep up with her.
I reached the bottom of the hill, and saw her climbing
up the path that led to the domim tree, climbing and
crying.

The preparations for the trip to Poland became the center of our lives. After our work and classes, we were
always busy with Yola's preparations. "So that she can go
in style," in the words of Sarah B.

And when Yola finally had the plane ticket in her
hands, we passed it from one to the other, feeling it,
touching it. We read all the little letters on the ticket. We
didn't skip over even one detail. We read the flight regulations, the insurance regulations, and even the weight of
the luggage that was allowed. The names of the cities that
she would pass over on the long journey to her father
really inspired our imagination. We gathered around her
while she held the ticket, and someone brought a big
world map and spread it out on the floor. We traveled
across oceans and continents, mountains and rivers, until
we reached Poland. That's where he was waiting for her.
A big circle in blue ink was drawn around the word
"Poland," and a big "X" in red ink was drawn alongside
the word "Warsaw."

Somebody suddenly called out in Polish, "*Pani Yola
Mintz. Proshe bardzo. Pani Yola Mintz*," which means *"Miss
Yola Mintz, please."*

And Yola said, "No, no. They'll surely call me by my

name as it's written in my passport: 'Yolanda, Yolanda
Mintz.' If my father hears, 'Yola,' he won't even know that
it's me. He won't even turn his head. Only here at the
village am I called Yola."

The girls who knew Polish began to show off, and
Yola, who had practically forgotten the language, said,
"Wait a minute, girls. Remind me how to say 'How are
you?' 'Where were you all these years?' and 'Hug me' and
'I love you.'" The girls immediately sat down and
refreshed her memory of the Polish language, giggling all
the time. Ayala and I stood by, watching almost like
strangers.

Yola was to fly from Tel Aviv to Zurich. Zurich to
Paris. And from Paris to Vienna. Vienna, the capital of
Austria. That's where Yola would have to stay overnight.
She was to sleep in a hotel in the city, and the next day, in
the morning, she'd get on a Polish plane that would take
her to Warsaw. I wondered how she would manage in
Vienna on her own. We were worried about her
encounter with the German language. Yola didn't want to
follow this route. She wondered if it was possible to bypass
Vienna. We tried to think of alternative routes, as if we
were experienced navigators. But we couldn't find any
other solution, so Yola had to accept her fate. She would
stay in Vienna as planned, and if anyone approached her
in German, she wouldn't respond. "As far as they're concerned, I'm deaf and dumb. And besides, I don't have
anything to say to those Austrians. I just have to get from
Vienna to Warsaw as quickly as possible!" she decided.

After Yola's travel plans were finalized, the only thing left to do was begin to pack. It took hours to pack the suitcase, which really wasn't so big. Never was one suitcase packed by so many people. The articles of clothing were packed in and taken out over and over again, spread on the floor and repacked. And the presents, too: a diary for her trip to Poland, which Alex bound especially for Yola, and a pair of wooden bookends in the shape of hands that he made for her. "I had a good piece of wood that was just right. I made them for your father," Alex had said. "Give them to him as a present from you."

When Yola wrapped the bookends, she said, "How did Alex know what was just right for my father? Our house was full of books. Books and more books. Walls filled with books." She buried the gift in the heart of the suitcase.

For a moment it was quiet, then Sarah B. said, "Yola, I'll arrange the notes, and you'll continue with the clothing." The notes and the envelopes with the requests for finding relatives in Poland were put into the suitcase. We saw Chavi put in a note of her own. She pretended that she had found it by accident, that it had fallen on the floor. And that way she was able to put it on the top of the pile that was placed into a brown paper bag that was buried among the clothes. The girls donated warm socks, warm underwear, undershirts, and sweaters. And pictures. Pictures of our youth village. So that her father could see and get to know it. So that he would know where she had been and wouldn't worry. We wanted him to know that it was good and beautiful here. We added a few group pictures of all of us, and the girls in the group, of Yola's friends. Including the funny one where the girls were making donkey ears over Yola's head, sticking their tongues out and crossing their eyes. That would make him laugh.

Yola's departure was only days away. The special clothes that we had prepared for her were already hanging from the window handle, and sitting underneath them were brightly polished shoes with white socks tucked inside of them. A sock folded into each shoe. It was as if a girl with no body and no face was hanging on the window.

"Yola, put the clothes on already," we urged. The packed suitcase was standing next to Yola's bed, and a heavy woolen coat was hanging over it, which was loaned to her by Ruth. "You've got to wear it, Yola," she had said, "it's cold there now." And when Yola stood there, with the coat casually draped over her, it was hard to tell whether she had just arrived from there, or whether she was waiting to head off for a long journey.

For three days and three nights it rained nonstop. "It's good for the crops," observed Ariel. "It's a very good year."

Wim was also very happy. "It's really like the climate of Europe," he said, meaning our recent weather.

I was worried about the seeds and bulbs that we had planted on the hill, which had already sprouted their first buds. A surplus of water was the same as a lack of

water—that's what they taught us. But Wim said, "It's
really good for the ones that are already in the ground.
They're used to a lot of rain. Just you wait. Soon. Pretty
soon you'll see the wonder."

After work and our classes we congregated in Yola's
room. We had abandoned our own rooms. For hours we
sat with Yola in her room, which had become the center
of our lives. We went back to our rooms only to sleep.
My roommates and I couldn't stand how our room
looked, with Mira's unmade bed standing in the middle,
with her body spread out on top of it. Mira wasn't invited to Yola's room, and she didn't try to come on her
own. Now it was clear to her that she was rejected and
hated by all of us.

We sat in Yola's room and talked almost always about
the influence of the weather on her upcoming trip. Were
strong winds good for the plane? Was it hard for the pilot
to fly the plane in the middle of such strong gusts and
rain? And if it was so rainy here, what would it be like
there, in Poland? The winter there must be terrible. We
compared everything that happened in our lives here
with the unknown that was about to happen there.

After three days of stormy rain, while we were sitting
in the classroom waiting for our teacher, Emanuel, the
sun suddenly appeared, bursting through the clouds. First
there was one ray, and then another and another. And
then the sunlight lit up the sky which had all at once
become clear.

Emanuel came into the classroom with a thick book

under his arm. "Children," he said, "open the windows. Let the beauty come in. What a beautiful day it is today." And after he gazed through the window at the sunlit sky, he continued, "Come on, let's go outside. On my way here, I saw an apple tree in bloom. Let's go to it. Today's a beautiful day for Dulcinea, Don Quixote's lover. We'll read about her there, underneath the apple tree."

We took the rolled up canvas, which stood ready just for this purpose in the corner of the room, and went out on our way to the apple orchard. Our feet became mired in mud, but the sun greeted our faces. After we spread the canvas out under the tree and sat on it, Emanuel asked us to be silent so that we could listen to the slight buzzing sound of the bees that were hovering above us, celebrating the end of the rain. Emanuel always insisted that we should keep our eyes and ears open to the movements of nature, that we shouldn't miss a thing. He taught us literature. But his love for nature knew no bounds, and we were all inspired by it.

A thick book lay on his lap, and his hand moved over the velvet, green cover with its golden illustrations. With great love, he turned the pages and began to read to us in his pleasant voice chapters from *Don Quixote* by Cervantes in the wonderful translation by Chaim Nachman Bialik, our national poet. Every so often he would stop and exclaim, "What a poet, what a wonderful translation. May Chaim Nachman be blessed." That's how we studied at the youth village. Mainly outside, in accordance with the seasons of the year. When the citrus fruits blossomed and their intoxicating fragrance reached our classroom, Emanuel would say, "The blossoms are calling us, children." And then we would go out to the orange grove and would study under the orange trees. When the apple trees blossomed, we sat in the orchard. There were classes that took place in the wheat fields, and we would be drowning in a sea of golden stalks before the harvest. Or we would be sitting near the little stream whose water trickled by the edge of the village in wintertime, beyond the hill. When the wadi would fill up and we could hear the gurgling of the water, we would go down to the wadi, dip our feet into its waters, and study.

We loved Emanuel and his very special classes. He was a poet who never read his poetry to us, but we knew his poems. Ariel had a subscription to a literary journal that published Emanuel's work, and he would read Emanuel's poems to us.

I wanted to remember this special time, these magical moments. To remember and not to forget. Ever since I had parted from my diary, I had begun to accumulate images, flavors, fragrances. So that I wouldn't forget them, so they wouldn't disappear. With my eyes, I scanned the faces of those who were sitting in a circle around Emanuel, like a hidden camera that saw everything: the leaves on the tree glistening after the rain, the transparent blossoms, the clear, biting air, the colors, the faces—everything. And I didn't want to forget the touch of Yurek's hand. For a whole hour he held my hand in his. And Emanuel, who saw everything too, smiled warmly and said, "I am a witness to your love." Even a crow that glided above the circle had something to say. It cried out in its hoarse voice and wouldn't stop. We laughed and imitated its voice. What does it want? Why does it insist on gliding here, next to us? Emanuel said, "Let him be. This crow is known as a great admirer of Cervantes, let him stay." But the bird seemed to be impatient, and it flew away from us, and after landing on the top of a cypress tree, it continued to cry out. Its voice grew louder, and once again it glided over us. This time, it brought some friends, two more black crows. What did they want?

Then we saw someone's image through the trees, appearing and disappearing. It was Ruth, the nurse, with her black rubber boots being sucked up into the mud, drawn in and pulled out, step after step. Heavy, hesitant steps. When she drew near us, wrapped in her big blue scarf over her white smock, she stopped and looked at us. Emanuel called to her, "Come here, Rutka. Sit down and join us in the joy of Cervantes." Ruth, who seemed to ignore his invitation, leaned over and whispered something into his ear. He got up and apologized to her, returned a minute later, and stood looking at us with his beautiful gray eyes. We saw him hesitate for a moment, fold his hands, open them, pull a leaf off the tree, squeeze it between his fingers, throw it away, cover his face with his hands, run his hands over his head, comb his light hair with his fingers, and once again look at us, hesitating.

Clearing his throat, he said, "Yola my dear, come here please. Ruth is waiting for you."

Yola, who was in a good mood, jumped up, shook the grass off her clothes, and ran toward Ruth. "I'll be right back," she said. "Emanuel, don't run too fast with Don Quixote. Wait for me." And we heard her laugh and say, "This mud, it can put the fear of God into you. You can really get stuck here."

We heard Ruth say solemnly, "Let's walk slowly, Yola. There's no reason to run."

Yola went with Ruth, and we returned to Emanuel. Only Emanuel didn't return to *Don Quixote*. He just sat there, staring at the sky, and suddenly he said, "Let's stop here. We'll respect Yola's request, and return to the sad knight and his Dulcinea in the next lesson." And then he let us go.

As always, the announcement of an early end to a class, or the sudden shortening of a lesson, aroused cries of joy. Alex and Zevick carried the canvas roll on their shoulders like a painting of grape bearers in biblical times, and they began to sing, "Our baskets are on our shoulders, our heads are covered with flowers."

Emanuel plodded after them in the mud, with a slow, heavy step, and he quietly said, as if to himself, "It shouldn't be that way. Maybe there shouldn't be any singing right now."

A freckled, red-haired girl stood in the corridor of the group's quarters and recited the words that she was supposed to say: "Ariel asks that you not wait for him. That you go to eat without him. He'll be late." Then she ran to her friend who was waiting for her at the entrance.

We managed to shout after her, "Hey, redhead, who asked you to give us the message?" But she didn't hear us, and she left with her friend. We went toward the dining room, strolling along, still filled with the sense of sudden freedom created by the shortened lesson.

Ariel never got to the dining room, to supper. Yola also missed the meal. She still had a lot of preparations to finish before her trip. In another forty-eight hours she would climb on to the plane that would take her to her father. Ever since she had the ticket in her hands and the date for the trip had been set, we were counting the days with her, as if we were counting the days till the harvest began. And now the final countdown had begun. Just another forty-eight hours were left until her departure, and so much more still had to be done. True, the suitcase was packed, the clothes were ironed and hanging from the window handle, and the ticket was safely in her drawer. So, what else was left to do? We didn't exactly know. But such a trip surely involved a lot of unanticipated things. When Yola didn't show up at the dining room, we prepared a tray filled with everything we had for supper, so that she wouldn't, God forbid, miss a meal. After all, she had to eat, had to have strength.

And then we heard the sound of the gong screeching in our ears as it split the air. We froze. Its heavy clang signified something bad. Something had happened.

Something terrible. And we didn't know what. The
sound of the gong was a signal calling us to gather
together immediately in the big hall. Like during a war,
we ran from the dining room into the big hall.

CHAPTER 8

The hall was filled with kids from wall to wall. We stood there, tense, waiting for Rachel. When the principal came into the big room, the way was cleared for her, and someone gave her a hand to help her onto the stage. She stood there, a tiny woman, dressed in a gray dress that gave an even paler look to her pale face. She asked the counselors to check to make sure that all the kids were there, and when they responded positively, she began to speak. "Dear children." She stopped speaking, took a deep breath, let out a sigh, and continued. "Pupils, teachers, and counselors—the Udim family." She waited for a moment, swallowed, and then continued in a weak voice, much weaker than usual. It was clear that she was having trouble speaking. "A deep sense of mourning has come over our home," she said. "Today, in the afternoon, we were informed from Poland that the father of Yola Mintz from the Sunflower group died last night in Warsaw. We don't know the exact details, but apparently his heart couldn't take the tremendous excitement he was feeling about the meeting he was going to have with his child, with our Yola." A hushed whisper spread through the hall, and Rachel didn't even ask for silence. She waited. She knew that we needed some time to digest the bitter message.

And then, a few minutes later, she said, "Children, nothing I can say can provide consolation for the loss. I'm sorry that I had to call you together so suddenly, but I felt that I had to say something this evening to prevent inaccurate rumors. Yola's sorrow is our sorrow, all of us." After a brief pause, she added, "There's nothing else I can say to you."

Someone began to cry at the edge of the hall, and someone else joined in, and then one of the girls who was standing close to the stage said, "Can I please ask a question?"

"Definitely," Rachel answered. "If you have any questions, please ask them."

"Does Yola know already?" the girl asked.

"Of course she knows," said Rachel. "Soon after the message arrived we told Yola. She's had a very difficult day. She's resting now." But before she had finished the sentence, the door to the hall opened and Yola came in accompanied by Ruth.

Silence settled over the hall, and all eyes turned toward the door. Ruth's hand was on Yola's shoulder, but Yola gently removed the hand and quietly made her way to the stage on her own. Yola climbed up onto the stage and turned toward us. She addressed us all: "I have here

a bag filled with a lot of notes with requests to find relatives in Poland. Where should I put it?"

"It's okay, Yola. I'll take care of it," Rachel said.

But Yola said, "No, no, Rachel. I'll give them back
the envelopes. It's all right." And then she began to take
the envelopes and the notes out of the big bag one by
one, calling the names in a weak voice, waiting a
moment, then surveying the packed hall. Someone
would raise a hand, and Yola would go to him or her in
total silence. We followed her movements throughout
the big hall. Wherever she went, the kids would move
apart and create a path for her.

One of the girls in the group whispered, "We've got
to put a stop to this. She still doesn't understand what
happened to her."

The strange ceremony continued for at least an hour,
but no one moved. I saw Ruth exchanging glances with
Rachel. Afterward, she came over to Yola, gathered up
the rest of the envelopes, put them back in the brown
bag, and whispered, "Come, Yola, come with me. That's
enough." Ruth coaxed her toward the door, and Yola followed her. Her hands lay limp at her sides, her face was
frozen, her eyes dry. And we held our breath. No one
moved.

Rachel turned toward us and said, "Dear children, I
know how hard this moment is for you. The counselors
are here, ready to talk with you. My door is also open. If
any of you wants to talk to me, please don't hesitate.
That's why we're here."

*   *   *

Night had fallen. We were in the shower room, almost all the girls in the group. No water flowed from the faucets, the sinks were free, and the long wooden bench was filled to capacity. Anyone who didn't find a place on the bench sat on the cold, dry floor.

For at least an hour we tried to calm Chavi, who hadn't stopped crying since we left the big hall. We were still trying to comfort her when her good friend Esty said, "Enough, Chavi. There's nothing we can do. Crying won't help," and then she began to cry as well.

Sarah B. was sitting, leaning against the wall, with her eyes closed. She didn't brush her hair or massage her face. She just sat there, helpless, like the rest of us. Every so often she'd whisper something, such as, "Put some water on her face" or "She should lie down in her room."

But Chavi insisted on staying with us in the shower room, mumbling, "Soon. Soon it will be over." From time to time she looked in the mirror above the sink and said, "Enough, damn it, I don't want to cry. I just can't control it." Then she would turn to us and say, "Look at my face, see how it's swelled up. My eyes are red, just like a rabbit's. I look terrible."

We sat there for some time, feeling helpless. The bitter message about the death of Yola's father had stunned us all. We just didn't know how to cope with the blow.

Then Chavi began to relax, her tears stopped streaming down her face, her shoulders began to sway, and her heavy breathing began to echo throughout the room. She wiped her nose with a towel, saying to herself, "I'm okay, I'm okay." It was quiet in the shower room. The silence began to calm us. We sat there, withdrawn into ourselves, like at a wake. And then we heard a thud, and afterward, the sound of a heavy object being dragged on the ground. We followed the dragging sound as it drew nearer and nearer. The door of the shower room opened, and Ruth was standing there with Yola. The heavy suitcase was in front of her, and she was pushing it forward with her feet, shove after shove. Yola stood in front of us, and Ruth said, "Girls, Yola insists on opening the suitcase and returning all the clothes that you gave her for the trip."

We looked at Ruth, and Ruth looked at us, as if she were asking for help. She had been spending hours with Yola, and Yola was really stubborn. Now she wanted to return the clothes, just the way she returned the notes and the envelopes in the big hall.

"Yola," we said, "there's no rush, it can wait." But she had already opened the suitcase, was sitting on the floor, and had begun to pull out the clothes, one piece at a time, calling our names. She knew exactly which item of clothing in the stuffed suitcase belonged to which girl, and we gave in. When she called someone's name, the girl would approach her to receive the item of clothing, which was folded up so nicely. For a moment it was possible to imagine that she had just returned from a long trip and was giving out the gifts that she had brought with her.

Ruth went over to the sink and washed her face. Sarah B. approached her and said, "Ruth, go get some rest. We'll manage. Don't worry, we'll help Yola."

Ruth hesitated for a moment, and then she approached Yola, who said to her, "Go ahead, Ruth. I'm okay. Can't you see? I'm just emptying out the suitcase, and that's that. It's over." Ruth went reluctantly toward the door, together with Sarah B., who continued to reassure her.

She left, and we looked at one another. Chavi turned away and began to cry again, and Yola asked, "Why is Chavi crying? Doesn't she feel well? Maybe we should help her," and she continued to rummage through her suitcase. When she pulled out some warm winter clothing, she spread it out in front of us and picked up the white woolen underwear and began to laugh. "Look what my aunt gave to me, *gatkes*, probably her husband's underwear, or her son's," she said. She got up from the floor. "I didn't even try them on," and she put them on over her khaki pants. She looked fat and ridiculous in the long woolen underwear, and she began to sway like a clown and wave in all directions, shouting, "She wanted me to meet my father in these clothes. My aunt must have gone completely mad." We were stunned. We had never seen Yola go wild. She was always withdrawn into herself, quiet. And now, she was in the midst of a grotesque dance, grabbing Naomi's woolen hat, which she had just returned to her, and Esty's big scarf, right out of their hands, laughing a strange laugh that quickly turned into a shriek. "To Poland! I ask you, is that how anyone travels to Poland? My father will run away if he sees me looking like this," she ranted. We all looked at Sarah B., expecting that she would put a stop to it. None of us had the courage to stop Yola.

Sarah B. approached her, and quietly said, "Yola. That's enough, come here. You're really tired now. I'll help you, and we'll finish unpacking the suitcase." Sarah B. took the clothes out of the suitcase, and the girls made room on the wooden bench for all the items of clothing. She gently took out the bookends and the diary that Alex had prepared, as if they were rare and expensive objects.

Yola noticed, and she took them from her, saying, "Oh, these belong to Alex. I have to give them to Alex Deutsch." She was just about to leave the shower room, dressed in those ridiculous clothes. We stopped her, and Sarah B. made some room on the bench and sat her down. She took the diary and the bookends from her, and then removed the hat from her head and the scarf from around her neck. Yola just sat there like a good little girl. Leaning against the wall, she lifted her feet, and Sarah B. began to pull off the long woolen underwear, one leg and then the other. Then Yola began to cry. Tears that soon turned into a heartrending wail. And then all the other girls who had managed to hold in the pain until now let loose, as well.

Mira arrived in the shower room with her washing kit, went over to the sink, and began to brush her teeth—the daily routine. She looked at us with scorn,

and said, "Why are you all wailing here, like babies? Go
cry under your stupid tree on the hill." Though we heard
her clearly, we didn't react. On her way out, she tossed
behind her, "What hysteria! After all, all those years she
thought that he was dead, right? So now she's sure." She
passed close to Yola, who was still crying, and said,
"Actually, it's for the best. Now at least you know exactly where he's buried, and maybe one day you'll even be
able to get to Poland to visit his grave."

We were shocked. Mira's words pounded against us.
"Get out of here, you monster! You hear me?" Sarah B.
shouted. Not holding back, Sarah B. struck her. Mira,
who wasn't prepared for the blow, tried to hit back, but
then all the girls jumped her and began to kick and pull
her hair. All the anger that we had been accumulating
was poured out on Mira. The girls pushed her under the
sink and continued to kick her. She tried to defend herself, covering her face with her hands, but they
continued to kick, pinch her arms, and hit her, vicious-
ly, accompanying the blows with screams and curses.
Among them were some curses in Polish, but I couldn't
make out who was shouting them. Mira didn't cry, and I
couldn't understand how she could take it. I stood on the
sidelines, bit my lip, and just looked on. I really wanted
to hit her. She certainly deserved it, without a doubt, but
I said to myself, "Don't get involved. Just watch and
remember this moment."

Suddenly, Mira began to rise. Yola said, "Wash your
face and go to your room." And Mira did as she was told.

She washed her face, picked up her towel and her toi-
letries, which were scattered all over the floor, and stuffed
them back into her washing kit. Yola accompanied her to
the door. "It's a real shame how we behaved. We almost
killed her," she reprimanded. The girls muttered, "Too
bad we didn't. She deserves it, that evil animal."

Yola knelt on her knees and closed the suitcase.
"Enough, girls," she said. "Let's go to sleep. Tomorrow
morning we have to go to work, and then to class. We've
got to get some rest." The girls dispersed, and I headed
back to my room.

Mira was sitting on her folding bed in the middle of
the room. Her face was puffed up. She caressed her
bruised left arm, brought it to her lips, and kissed her
cuts. *She's licking her wounds*, I thought.

"What bad animals, those girls. Look what they did
to me," Mira said when I came in. She pointed to her
injured arm. "I could have killed them if I wanted to. I'm
strong enough. I can kill if I want to," she said. I was
silent, still stunned by what had happened in the shower
room. Mira continued, "What did I say? That now at
least she's certain that her father's dead. If you think
about it, she's lucky. Now she'll have a place. A grave that
she can visit. There'll be a tombstone. How many of us
in the group have had a grave that we can visit?"

"A grave to visit . . . ," those words kept echoing in my
head, not letting go.

"Are you with me? I'm talking to you," Mira said.
"Say something."

"You're right," I said, "it's the most important thing. There must be a grave." I ran out of the room. I didn't want to talk to anyone, didn't want to deal with what had happened. Mira had put her finger on the thing that had been bothering me all these past few days. I realized that I had to find my father's grave. This Mira, I might one day even thank her for this discussion.

I made my way to the hill. When I began to climb the path that led to the domim tree, I saw that someone was already there. For some reason, I was sure that it was Yurek and called his name. "It's not Yurek," came the response, "it's me, Zevick. I'll be right down." I quickly left the path and sat down on a broken tree stump at the foot of the hill, sat and waited.

The moon peeking from behind the clouds poured forth slivers of pale light, and I could see Zevick beginning to disappear from sight. I thought, *Poor Zevick, he also came here to cry, just like me. Just like dogs, we run away to cry, to make sure that no one sees us in our moment of weakness.*

Once the tree was free, I climbed the path leading to it as fast as I could. The crisp night air filled my lungs. "I've got to," I said out loud, knowing that no one would laugh at me for talking to myself. After all, that's why I came up here, to my tree, despite my fear of the dark. "I've got to find my father's grave. I've got to have a place where I can go to visit him, to speak to him. It's really important to have a grave to go to." I spoke and the tree listened. Now that I was orphaned from my diary, all that was left was my domim tree. There wasn't a single person to whom I could speak about everything with complete honesty, the way I spoke to my diary. Not Ayala, not even Yurek. I couldn't tell Yurek how much I loved him. Once I had tried to tell him how he changed my life. When I first arrived at the youth village, I was sure that I was the most miserable girl around. Only after I met Yurek and his friends did I realize that I was better off than they were. Mother had always said to me, "Whenever things are going bad for you, look around. You'll always find someone who is worse off, someone who needs you."

So there was Yurek, who admitted that he needed me. And Yola, who was so battered by fate. And me, what did I really need? Just to find my father's grave.

Still enjoying my solitude, I suddenly heard a voice, "Is anyone up there? It's hard to see, say something."

"Yes, yes. I'm here. I'll be right down. Just a minute," I responded. And I thought, *What's happening to everyone tonight? How come they're all arriving at such a late hour?* I delayed for another minute, but realized that I would have to give up my place under the tree. On my way down, it became clear to me that I wouldn't be able to postpone it any longer. I had to find my father's grave.

That night I took out the brown envelope with my father's picture in it and hid it under my pillow. The next day, I told Yurek about my plan. "I'm going to find it. His grave," I said.

"Where will you go?" asked Yurek. "You have no idea where he's buried. Where will you begin?" I showed him the picture that my aunt had sent me. When he saw my father's face, he said, "Look how young he is, like a child. And you look so much like him, it's amazing." He turned the picture over and read the words that were written on the back.

"What do you think, Yurek?" I asked. "What do those words mean, 'Kaibeach Haifa'?"

Yurek didn't know. "Maybe it's the name of somebody in Haifa."

"That's it," I said. "I've got to begin in Haifa. I'll go there and start looking. I won't stop until I find it."

Yurek looked at me with his narrow penetrating eyes, and said, "I don't want you to be disappointed. I'm worried about you. Haifa is a big city. How are you going to find your father's grave in such a huge city? Maybe we should try to talk to your mother. Maybe she'll talk to me. I can speak to her in Polish," he said, and laughed. "Maybe she'll understand better in Polish, your mother, and she won't be so difficult."

Suddenly, I found myself defending my mother. "No, Yurek," I said, "that's not the problem. My mother is very sick. Her soul was really damaged by everything that she went through. Just try to imagine, she can't even utter my father's name. Once I heard her crying out in her sleep 'Max, Max,' and I knew that that was his name. Days went by before she admitted that his name was really Max and that she still dreamed about him at night.

I just can't know what goes on in her head when I bother her with my questions, when I try to make her tell me about him. I really pity her so much." When I spoke about her like that, with Yurek, I was overwhelmed with longing for Mother and wanted to see her.

For a moment, I stopped talking, and Yurek pleaded with me, "Don't hold it all in, talk to me. We're friends, aren't we? That's why I'm here."

"Yurek, I'll find him, you'll see. I'll find him," I said.

Once again, Yurek offered to join me in the search, and I refused. "You're so stubborn," he said, "and won't let me help you. Why?"

And later he asked if he could accompany me to the main road. "Only up to the gate," I said. "I want to make the whole trip on my own."

I told Ayala that I was going to the most important meeting of my life, and she asked, "You and Yurek, are the two of you planning something?"

"No. It has nothing to do with Yurek. It's my father," I answered, and got her to swear that she wouldn't say a word about it to anyone. I told her that I would leave tomorrow morning and would return only after I had accomplished the mission that I had taken upon myself. "Don't worry, Ayala," I reassured her. "You know me. I'll be all right."

"Promise that you won't hitch rides," she said, and gave me some money for a bus. "Everyone says that it's not as safe as it used to be."

I didn't argue with her, and also didn't promise anything. I put my blue pants under the mattress, so that they would be ironed overnight, and my white embroidered blouse on the chair near my bed. Those were my Sabbath clothes. I polished my brown shoes until they shined. I never devoted so much attention to my clothes as I did that evening. I placed my flowerpot, with its beautiful forget-me-nots which had already bloomed, on the chair. I knew that this would be an important day in my life, and I planned for it accordingly.

In the morning, I started off on my way, with the flowerpot in my hand. Yurek accompanied me to the gate, and before we parted, he rested his hand on my shoulder, and said, "You're doing the right thing. I envy you." And he didn't say another word. He just shook my hand and turned back toward the village.

CHAPTER 9

I stood at the edge of the main road and waited for the first vehicle that would pick me up. I would either take a bus or hitch a ride; after all, I had made no promises to Ayala. A bus arrived, and halted at the bus stop. "Where are you going, child?" asked the driver.

"To Haifa," I said.

"Come on, get in." When the bus began to move, I was still standing, counting the coins for the ticket, and I suddenly lurched forward and grabbed the driver's seat. The seat behind him was empty, so I sat down. And then he began to ask me, "Where in Haifa? Up on the mountain, or down near the port?"

I didn't know what he meant. "I'm not really sure," I mumbled.

"Haifa's a big city," he said. "Maybe I can help you."

I leaned close to him and whispered, "I'm looking for someone I don't know and don't know how to find." I spoke very quietly. A few other passengers stared at me, and I felt ridiculous—a passenger who doesn't know where she's going.

The driver urged me on. "Don't worry. I'm from Haifa, and I know the city like the back of my hand."

"I'm looking for someone... named Kaibeach," I said.

He looked at the road ahead of him, and then turned and said, "Kaibeach? A man named Kaibeach? How can he live with such a name? The Haifa cemeteries are called Kaibeach."

I cut him off, "That's it, exactly! That's where I have to go."

"I see," he said. "And that pretty flowerpot, you're bringing it there?"

Before I had a chance to answer, a voice was heard from the back of the bus, "Driver, stop talking with the young girl and concentrate on the road."

The driver looked in the mirror above his head, smiled at me and said, "You're right, mister."

The driver stopped talking, and we continued in silence. At the Hadera junction, a few more people got on the bus, and the driver seemed to remember my presence. "Excuse me," he said, "but I'm an amateur gardener, and I don't recognize the plant in your flowerpot."

"*Vergeet mij niet*," I said, "a Dutch plant. It's given to someone who you want to remember you and not to forget. It's called 'forget-me-not' in Hebrew." We continued on our way. Every so often, the melody he was humming under his thick mustache grew louder, and it seemed to accompany us throughout the long journey.

When the Carmel mountains began to appear, he said, "Child, we're getting closer. That's Haifa." And a few minutes later he said, "This is it. That's where Kaibeach begins." To the right of the bus, on the side of the road, was a huge field filled with white crosses.

"I'll get off here," I said.

He stopped. Before I got off, I plucked a flower from my vase and gave it to him. He laughed. "I won't forget you," he said. "But tell me, what's your name?"

I said, "Aviya, that's my name."

"Aviya? That's a strange name." He smiled and continued on his way. I stood there at the spot where I had gotten off and took a deep breath.

I turned toward the cemetery. At the entrance, I stopped for a moment. I was afraid to go in on my own. There was something really frightening about the silence, the only sound being the whizzing of cars going by on the main road. I said to myself, "Don't be afraid. Come on. It's now or never." And I entered with slow and hesitant steps.

It was a strange place. A sea of white crosses was everywhere, with names written in a foreign language. I passed among the graves and thought, *How will I find anyone here? And why here? After all, this is a Christian cemetery. Maybe I'll find some Jewish tombstones in the back.* I didn't know how much time had passed since I had gotten off the bus. I moved back and forth among the graves, all of which looked very much alike. Crosses, tons of white crosses, and not a single Jewish name. I wondered, *Who*

are these Christians? So many foreign Christians died here,
when did it happen? And all that time, I didn't see a living
soul. There was no one to talk to.

Opposite the cemetery was the sea. I could hear the
waves breaking on the rocks and feel the taste of the salt
coming from the water. The weather was kind to me that
day, and the sky was clear. I continued on my journey
among the foreign cemeteries, looking for my father's
grave. The last cemetery that lay alongside the main road
was a Jewish cemetery. Finally. In front of it stood a big
iron gate with a Star of David on top and a few beggars
shaking some tin cans. "Charity will save from death.
Charity will save from death," they said, revealing
mouths without teeth.

I didn't have anything to give them. I didn't know
which way to turn. So I asked them, "Where should I
start? Where do the graves begin?"

An old woman came up to me as I passed through
the gate and said in broken Yiddish, "*Dorten, dorten,* there,
there."

I walked for at least an hour among the tombstones,
down the twisted paths that seemed to lead in all directions. I reached the military section. I recognized it by
the Israeli army symbols that were etched into the tombstones. Rows and rows of stones, with Hebrew names
etched into them. Here and there I saw people leaning
against the tombstones, and I could hear the sound of
quiet prayer in the air. Or maybe it was the sound of
someone crying? I was afraid to approach the people, but

a woman in black rose up from a tombstone, wiped her tears away, and asked, "Who is it? A brother? A father?"

"A father," I said.

"Was he in this unit?" she asked. But I didn't understand what she meant. "Where was he killed? When? In which battle?"

All I could say was, "It was a long time ago. He died a long time ago. Before I was born."

And the woman said, "How could it happen before you were born? You can't die..." She immediately apologized. "Everything can happen. When the one up there decides to take, he takes, even from babies who haven't been born yet. You're in the wrong place, child. This is for the army. Don't you see? These are army graves. The old graves from years ago are over there, in the other direction. Close to the gate."

I turned around and headed back. When I got to the gate, the beggars came toward me, once again crying, "Charity will save from death. Charity will save from death." I was afraid of them. Why couldn't they leave me alone? After all, I didn't have anything to give them. I don't know what drew me toward the burial section near the left side of the entrance. *I'll start looking here*, I thought, and began passing through the rows of identical graves. There were groups of little tombstones, and in the middle stood one taller tombstone—a big, tall cone made of light marble with dark veins, with the words FOR YOUR SAKE WE WERE KILLED engraved in big, black letters. Around it were iron rods and a rusty chain with

thick links that surrounded the big marble tombstone. I
passed by the rows of stone time after time. Again and
again. Something seemed to be guiding me from within. As if a hidden hand were leading me.

Four times I passed by the rows of stone. Four times
I passed by the tombstone with my father's name
engraved on it, and I didn't notice his name. The stones
darted before my eyes; I was dizzy. Stones, stones. Rows
of stones and white crosses all jumbled together.
Suddenly, everything became clear, and I finally recognized my father's name engraved in the marble.

On a gray, cracked marble tombstone, his name was
etched in letters that were blackened by sand and dust.
The marble slab was lying on· eight square rocks, and
wild grass was growing between them. Without realiz-
ing it, I had leaned over the slab and begun to pull out
the wild grass, stalk after stalk. My hands seemed to
move by themselves. I sat there, totally apathetic. My
eyes were dry, and I didn't cry. *What's happening to me?* I
wondered. *What's all the excitement? Where's the feeling of
the greatest moment in my life?* I pulled out all the wild
grass and piled it up on a little mound, and then I began
to clean the stone slab with my hands. Afterward, I wet
a handkerchief with my spit and began to clean the letters. Letter after letter. Slowly but surely, scraping out
every letter with my fingernails, and then wiping it with
the handkerchief. My mouth was dry, and the handkerchief, which was once clean and white, became gray and
dirty. I finally reached the final letter in my father's long,

foreign name. I scraped and scraped, and then it happened. A flood of tears burst forth, and my body began to shake. I kissed the cold stones and a wave of warmth overwhelmed me. At last, I knew that I had found him, and I remembered Mira's words: "The most important thing is a grave, a place to visit." I took the flowerpot full of forget-me-nots and leaned it against the marble slab. The thin, sturdy branches filled with the little flowers added color to my father's engraved name, a name that no one spoke, a name almost completely forgotten. I placed a little rock next to it, and then another one, just as I saw on the other graves. Now my father's tombstone also had a flower and some rocks. He wouldn't be alone anymore.

For at least an hour I sat next to father's tombstone, which sparkled with cleanliness, and I spoke to my father. I spoke out loud, without hesitation or inhibition. I told him about my mother, the woman he once loved and who loved him. And about the sorrow that had overwhelmed her soul ever since he died one day and left her alone without him. I told him that I didn't know why or how he died. I didn't understand why the tombstones alongside his were identical or who was buried next to him. "Help me," I said, "Watch over Mother, Father. She's very sick. And watch over me," I asked. "I need someone to take care of me." I told my father things that I always knew I would tell him when I met him. I wanted him to know me, so that I wouldn't be a stranger to him. "Father, I came to you. Look at me, it's me, your little girl," I said. I knew that from now on, I would come here again and again, that this was our place.

It was almost evening when the graveyard gardener approached me, riding on his squeaking bicycle, dragging a rake and a shovel behind him. "Young girl, you've been here for hours. I've seen you wandering around, and now it's almost closing time," he said. My eyes must have given away some of the excitement that I was feeling. "Is that your father?" he asked gently, and I nodded my head yes.

Then I said, "You're the gardener here, aren't you? Could you please water my flowers?"

"In the winter, God will do it better than I can, believe me," he said. "And if your beautiful plant makes it through the spring, I'll take care of it. I promise." He looked at the flowers in the flowerpot and touched them tenderly. "It's really pretty, your plant. I don't recognize this flower."

"Forget-me-not," I said.

"No, I'm sure I won't forget," he said.

I laughed and said, "No, no. That's the name of the flower. Forget-me-not. *Vergeet mij niet*, it's Dutch."

"You see, I learned something new," he said. "Forget-me-not. A beautiful flower. Just right for a cemetery." He laughed to himself and went on his way.

The next morning in the shower room, the girls asked, "Where did you disappear to yesterday?"

"I didn't disappear, I went to a family affair," I said.

"Happy or sad?" somebody asked.

"Happy. Very happy," I answered.

It was only then that I noticed that the girls were still gloomy and depressed. Then Yola came in, and I remembered her tragedy. Yesterday, I was totally immersed in my own life. I got really angry at myself, remembered how Mother always claimed that I was selfish, thought only about myself, and not about others.

"Girls, what's all this mourning?" Yola said. "It can't go on this way. We've got to continue to live. If we don't get a hold of ourselves, we'll really crack up." Yola's words gave strength to others. It was astonishing to see how Yola was changing right in front of our eyes. Where did she find this incredible strength? She was always so pale, such a weakling. So childish, dragging her Lalka pillow around with her. And now, it was as if she had grown up overnight.

Mira came in to wash herself, and she stood next to me, her face still all puffed up. I asked her, "How do you feel this morning? Does it still hurt?"

Silence settled over the shower room, and she glared at me with her evil eyes. "Since when do you care? Why are you suddenly asking me?" she said.

Ayala pulled me away from the sink and said, "Soon you'll be having heart-to-heart sessions with her. Why in the world are you talking to her?"

I wanted to say that if I could, I would have hugged her, because I felt that I owed her a lot. The things that she said to me that night after she was beaten up had inspired me to go find my father, and now that I had found him, I wanted to thank her. I thought that, but I didn't say a word.

I left the shower room. And once again, I had the feeling that all eyes were on me and every word I said was being placed under a magnifying glass. This invasion into my privacy was really starting to bother me. Sarah B. had expressed it so well during the big argument over the reparations: "I want to be alone, to get up alone, to go to sleep alone, alone, alone, and not with four other girls. And not with everyone, and not always together." That morning, I wanted to be alone. And I wanted to run to him again, to my father, to the place where he was. There were so many things that I still hadn't managed to say to him. I wanted to see the tombstone again, to make sure it was still clean. And that the flower was still blooming.

But Ayala and Yurek stopped me from going. "Wait a while," they said. "You can't leave the village any time you want. You're lucky that nothing happened this time."

At the entrance to the dining room, Ariel stopped me and quietly said, "Please, I'm asking you, don't do that again. Not that way. Not without permission." I apologized, but didn't promise anything.

CHAPTER 10

A few minutes later Wim Van Fliman arrived, smiling and in good spirits. His eyes were shining and he begged my forgiveness. "Just one minute, okay? I want just to speak with Ariel."

I went inside and sat down at my table, and a minute later Ariel and Wim came in. Ariel said, "Gang, can I have your attention? Wim...uh, Tuviah...wants to say something to you."

And in his awkward language, Wim said, "Well, okay. Good morning, friends. The wonder is already here. I promised that..." He looked around and around and asked, "Well, how do you say I promised and now it's here? It is? I kept my promise." His words rang out all over the dining room. "I kept my promise," repeated Wim. "So, all of you, please, come before work, just for a few minutes, to the hill. See you all soon," and he waved his hand and went on to the other dining rooms.

After breakfast we all made our way to the hill, and then we saw the wonder in all its glory. Our hill had blossomed into a dazzling array of colors. I had never seen such beauty before. Flowers of every shade and color, the likes of which we had never seen, like a rainbow. Huge tulips, narcissuses, hyacinths, and also forget-me-nots. Our hill looked like a splendid embroidered dress, checkered with precious stones. We stood there, dumbfounded by the extraordinary beauty, and we applauded.

We didn't think that it was strange to clap our hands for a bunch of flowers, for the hill, for nature. Handsome Avner Engel from the twelfth grade climbed to the top of the hill, stood in front of us, and as he straightened his sturdy legs, he said, "Gang, I think that Wim and his friends in the Dutch underground deserve a tremendous round of cheers from us. Let them hear us from the main road." And then Avner thundered in his big voice, "To the members of the Dutch underground and Wim Van Fliman—hip! hip!"

"Hooray!" we answered. And again, "Hip! Hip! Hooray!" We shouted at the top of our lungs. Our voices really carried.

Then Avner said, "And now let's all sing together, one, two, three." His hands moved as if he were lifting the heavy accordion to his chest and pretending to play it. All the kids who were usually in charge of playing the recorder started marching in a row up the path toward the top of the hill, carefully making sure that they didn't step on any flowers. They moved up the hill, and following Avner Engel's movements, they played beautiful

music on their imaginary instruments. Avner led us, and
we all began to sing with great gusto, "How beautiful is
the spring, in the field, in the meadow, when the flowers
bloom." And then we sang, "Who won't recognize us,
the tulip flowers." These were spring songs. And our
singing, on that wonderful spring morning, was really so
sweet. Our voices were floating in the air. I looked at Yola
and saw that she was singing. And I was singing too, like
everyone else. For some reason, I remembered what
Mother always used to say: "It's not good to sing in the
morning; it always ends in tears." I stopped, and just
moved my lips, as if I were still singing.

I gave myself over totally to the beauty of nature that
was celebrating together with us the joy of the blossom-
ing that symbolized the coming of spring. Songbirds
landed on the branches of our domim tree and joined in
the song, and fabulous butterflies and bees circled over
the flowers that covered the wonderful hill. Only Mira
stood off on the side, alone, isolated, and cut off from the
happiness. No one approached her, and no one asked her
to join us. She stood there on her own, as if she had been
punished, as if she had been forbidden to come near us.

When we finished the song, Avner said, "Gang, without even consulting the pupils' committee, I propose that
from now on we call this hill 'The Dutch Hill,' in honor
of the members of the Dutch underground. Who's in
favor?" We all raised our hands, and Avner said,
"Accepted by unanimous consent." Wim Van Fliman
came forward, together with his seven children, and they

concluded the festivities with a happy Dutch song that made them laugh, and made us laugh as well, despite the fact that we didn't understand a word. And so, in really good spirits, we started down the hill, each to his own place of work.

Word of our hill traveled great distances. People began to come from all over, just to see the wonder. They would come, armed with cameras, to take pictures of the hill and its elegant dress. They would ask, "What are those rare flowers? Where do they come from?" Alex prepared a wooden sign with an arrow and words etched in black, TO THE DUTCH HILL, which was placed near the main road on the path that led to the youth village. At the top of the hill he put another big, beautiful sign made of natural wood on which was written THE DUTCH HILL. A GIFT FROM THE MEMBERS OF THE DUTCH UNDER-GROUND TO THE CHILDREN OF UDIM.

On Sabbath afternoon, Yurek ran toward me, happily crying out, "People have come for you. You've got visitors."

I was surprised. "Visitors, for me? How come?" I asked. After all, I wasn't exactly used to visits.

"They asked for you," he said. "They asked for the longest braid in the Sunflower group."

We went together to the gate, to receive the visitors. There I recognized the Dotan family who had once given me a ride to the village. The father and mother with their little son and their daughter with the small, ridiculous thin braid that was hanging on the back of her head. They came armed with a camera, and when I approached them, they said, "We heard about your hill and came to see it." I proudly showed them our hill, and the domim tree, and I called each flower by its full name. The woman said, "It really is more beautiful during the day. When we brought you here at night, the place looked so frightening, but it's really pretty here during the day."

When I gave them a tour of the village and passed by a few groups of children, the girl said, "You don't look at all like orphans. You look just like regular kids."

Her mother grabbed her hand and whispered, "Nili, stop it. Watch what you say." And all I wanted to do was laugh, but I thought about what my mother would say at a moment like this: "There's no one to laugh with."

The Dotan family was already settled in their car, and at the moment that I was about to say good-bye to them, I suddenly said instead, "Could you take me with you? I've got to go see my mother."

"Is that how it works here, you leave whenever you want to?" the woman asked.

I lied to her. "That's the way it is on the Sabbath. We can leave whenever we want to, wherever we want to; we just have to return by evening." I crowded into the backseat.

The father had trouble starting the car, and I sat there afraid that someone might pass by and see me. *I just hope they don't catch me*, I thought. *I've got to get away to see my mother.* I so wanted to see her, ever since I ran away from her house during that sad visit. I so missed her and wor-

ried about her. I bent down so that I wouldn't be seen
and pretended that I was tying my shoelaces. Mr. Dotan
solved the problem, and we were on our way.

We approached the town. I asked to get off at the
spot where they had picked me up the first time. I said
good-bye to them and rushed to Mother. I ran quickly
and confidently. This time I knew the way. When I
arrived, I found that the house was locked. Friday afternoon, before the Sabbath, and Mother wasn't home? I
banged on the door. "Mother, Mother!" I shouted.

I ran to the other side of the house, climbed up on
the windowsill, and looked in. "Mother, Mother," I continued to cry.

A neighbor who lived next door to Mother came out
and said, "You're her daughter, right? We looked for you
and didn't know where to find you. You know, you
should leave us an address, a telephone number, either
yours or someone else's, so that we'll know where to find
you."

"What happened?" I asked in a panic. "Where's my
mother?"

She took me inside her house. "Not outside," she
said. "They don't have to hear everything." We stood in
the living room of her apartment, which was flooded
with light. A big table in the center of the room was covered with a white tablecloth and in the middle were two
shiny silver candlesticks. There was a smell of something
cooking, something really appetizing in the air. I wanted
to sit down for a moment, but my mother's neighbor

didn't invite me, she just closed the door and said, "She's in the hospital. They put her in about a week ago. My husband called the doctor; they came and they took her. Poor thing."

"Where is she, where did they take her?" I asked.

The neighbor squirmed, and finally she said in a very quiet voice, "You know...the hospital for the...soul... you know, a mental hospital."

I was about to leave the apartment, when the neighbor, whose name I didn't even know, stopped me. She called her husband, Aryeh. He said, "You can't go there on the Sabbath. They won't let you in. It's not a regular hospital, it's closed, you know." He looked at his wife, and after both of them looked at me, he offered to take me to my mother. "Someone's got to come with you," he said. I wanted to hug him.

Aryeh drove me to the hospital, which was in the next town. Throughout the ride, he didn't bother or question me, he just respected my silence. And when we arrived, he went into the reception room, spoke to the nurse, and she led me to Mother, by way of a long, narrow corridor with strange paintings in strong colors hanging on the walls. When we passed a group of patients, the nurse said to me, "Don't be afraid, they won't do anything to you. Just follow me." I didn't tell her that I had visited a hospital like this before. I thought, *How similar these hospitals are.*

"You can stay with her for a few minutes," she said. "It really makes no difference to her."

I didn't exactly understand what the nurse meant
until I stood very close to Mother. She was sitting on a
chair near her bed, as if someone had left her there and
forgotten her. Her beautiful eyes were glazed, and they
just stared into space. She was wearing a light blue
smock, and her hands were slumped at her sides. Even
after I bent down and said, "Mother, Mother," and wanted to kiss her, she didn't respond. Only her lips moved.

I heard her say, "Nurse, nurse," in a feeble voice.

The nurse looked at me and said, "There's no point.
It's not worth it for you to be here."

I ignored the nurse's words, and stayed with my
mother. I brushed her hair, and opening her drawer, I
took out a little bottle and put a few drops of perfume
on her. I painted her lips red, just the way she liked it.
She let me make up her face, without reacting. I hugged
her and put her hand on my head. The hand dropped off.

The nurse, who was watching, said, "It's a shame
you're going through all that effort. She doesn't recognize you. Come." The nurse accompanied me to the exit
and delivered me over to Aryeh. For some reason, she
spoke to him, not to me. "It will take some time," she
said. "She's being well taken care of, but this is really a
difficult period. We need a lot of patience."

How much patience do I need, how much patience, I
thought, *for her to get well? What good is patience if she's still
sick?*

"Where should I take you?" asked Aryeh, after we
were back in the car. "Home?"

"No," I said. "I want to go back to the youth village."

"I began this project, and I'll finish it," he replied. He drove me back to the village.

At the entrance I ran into two people. "Do you know Miriam Segal?" they asked me.

For a moment I didn't know who they meant. Miriam Segal? "There's a Mira Segal with us, who lives with me in our room," I said.

"Yes, yes," they said, "Mira Segal. Where is she?" I led them to the group's quarters. They sat on Mira's messy bed, which stood as usual in the middle of the room. They just sat there, not exchanging a word.

I said to them, "She's working now in the chicken coop. Do you want me to call her?"

"Yes, yes," they said. "Please call her." I went to the chicken coop to tell Mira that she had visitors.

Mira was busy gathering the eggs. She had just finished collecting all the eggs in one section. When I arrived, she had a pail filled with eggs in each hand. I went in, making my way among the hundreds of hens that squawked all around me, raising a tremendous ruckus. "You've got visitors," I called out. "Mira, people have come to see you."

She turned her head toward me. "What do you mean?"

"Don't you understand? You've got a visit. Guests have come to see you," I said.

She responded, "I can't have any visitors, don't be ridiculous."

I still managed to say, "What's wrong with you? I'm telling you that you have visitors."

But she just grumbled, "I don't have visitors, and no one ever comes to see me." She continued on past me.

"You don't want to listen to me? Who cares," I said, and started heading out toward the wire gate.

She stopped me. "Who came?" she asked.

"Two people. A man and a woman," I said.

"What do they look like?" she asked.

I found it hard to describe them. "I don't know. Not tall, sort of short…" And before I had even finished the sentence, she dropped the two pails filled with fresh eggs, and they splattered all over the ground. She opened the wire gate and ran out of the chicken coop, catching me completely off guard. The hens attacked the broken eggs and began to peck among all the shells and their spilt contents. When I managed to finally break free from them, I saw Mira racing toward the fields. "Mira, what's going on?" I called after her. "What should I tell them? They're waiting for you." She didn't answer but just kept running until she disappeared into a giant wheat field. She was gone, as if she had been swallowed up by the earth.

Why did I bother? I thought. *Why did I drag myself out to her, all the way to the chicken coop? And what should I do now? What should I tell those people? And the girls, they should never know about this. After all, we ostracized Mira.*

In thinking it over, I realized that my friend Ayala would never forgive me for having done something for "the monster." We had stopped calling her "her," or "that

one," or "that Mira." She was just "the monster." We
really hated her. But I just couldn't forget the things that
she had said to me about the importance of a grave
before I went out to look for my father's.

When I returned to the room, the two strangers were
still sitting on Mira's bed. Now I could get a look at
them and try to understand what had frightened Mira so
much. They sat there on the bed in the middle of the
room, close to each other. The man was thin, his face
gaunt, his eyes were sunk deep into their sockets, and his
lips were very narrow. He wore gray pants that looked
too big for him and a dark jacket that knew better days.
On his head he wore a black beret. There was something
absurd about that shriveled head, wearing the hat, with
bits of hair peeking out from behind his ears.

The woman wore a dark, almost black coat, which
was a bit faded. A black scarf, which surrounded her tiny
face, was tied under her chin. She really was little. When
she sat on the bed, her feet barely reached the floor, and
they were covered with white bandages under her baggy,
colorless socks. Sitting there, waving her legs back and
forth, she looked like a little girl. She was constantly
squeezing a white handkerchief between her fingers.

The room was filled with smoke. A cigarette dangled
from the corner of the man's mouth, and from time to
time he put the ashes out in a vase that he held in his
hand. His fingers were really bony and yellow. It's lucky
that Ayala didn't see him holding her beautiful vase. The
vase that her mother gave her before she died had been

converted into an ashtray by Mira's guest.

I stood in front of the strangers and didn't even stam-
mer when I said, "I'm sorry, I made a mistake. I went to
the chicken coop, but she wasn't there. She left this
morning with a bunch of kids on a trip to the north, and
they'll be back late this evening. I'm surprised," I said,
"that they didn't tell you this in the office when you
arrived. They should have known."

The two of them looked at each other and whispered
together in a foreign language. Afterward they got up.
Before they left, I said, "If you want to give her whatever you brought, you can leave it here. It will make her
happy."

And they said, "Who says we brought anything? We'll
come back another time." *What strange people*, I thought.
They come to visit a girl in a children's village, empty-handed.

They went on their way, and I immediately changed
the water in Ayala's vase. I placed the flower, which the
man had put on the floor, back in the vase, near her bed,
so that she wouldn't notice that anything had happened.

Soon after they left, the girls came back to the room.
Ayala said, "What's that strange smell? The room is filled
with smoke. It's really suffocating in here." She went to
the window and opened it. "Let's let some air in," she
said. "It's really disgusting in here." And I explained that
some visitors had come looking for Mira, and then they
had left. I didn't tell them that I had gone to tell Mira
and that she had run away.

CHAPTER 11

O nly when evening came and Mira still hadn't returned did I tell the girls what had happened in the chicken coop. When Ariel arrived to take us to supper, I told him the whole story. "Please keep this to yourselves," he said. "Let's not create a panic. Though, of course, I'll tell the guards and Rachel."

During the meal, no one asked about Mira. No one even noticed that she was missing. After the dining room emptied out, we put some food on a tray for her. Chavi and Esty were the first to leave the dining room, to make sure that the corridor was empty, that the coast was clear. We didn't want to run into any of our friends in the group and have to answer any questions. We kept the secret, kept our promise to Ariel. The hours went by, and still there was no sign of Mira. We began to get worried. We had no idea what had made her react that way. It was already lights-out time, the "pregnancy parade" of all the diary keepers was over, and we were the only ones still awake. "We won't go to sleep," we said, "not tonight. We'll wait for her."

Ariel begged us to go to sleep. "I'll stay up. Don't worry," he said. But we refused; we insisted that he leave the room and that he go and wait in his own room. We stayed up, and without even having discussed it, opened the window, took the linen off her bed, shook it out, and remade her bed. We stretched out the sheet and put the pillow and the blanket in their places. Chavi folded Mira's pajamas, so that they looked as if they had just been ironed. Her bed had never looked so clean and tidy. We spread out an embroidered napkin on the tray and put her supper on it. And I put Ayala's little vase right next to the tray, just like at Aunt Alice's house. We hated Mira, but suddenly we were worried about her and prayed that nothing bad would happen to her. We wanted her to come back. Time kept passing, and still there was no sign of her. Every so often Ariel would knock lightly on the door. He would come in and say, "Girls, that's enough. I appreciate your concern, but don't over-do it." Still, we didn't go to sleep. When one of us would be on the verge of collapsing, we'd wake her up. We wanted to be awake. We wanted to wait for Mira until she returned. And when she returned, it was important for her to know that we had worried about her. It was as if all our hatred had vanished.

It was almost morning when the door opened. Mira stood there for a moment, looking at us with astonishment. She asked, "How come you got up so early?"

"We didn't just get up. We never slept, we waited for you," Ayala said.

She didn't react, she just sat down on a chair. Then she asked, "Who made my bed?"

"We did," we said.

"And the food, who brought the tray?" Mira asked.

"We brought it," we said. "It's for you, we were worried about you."

She was silent, and while she was still sitting there, her eyes closed and her head slumped down on her shoulders. We laid her down on her bed, put the pillow under her head, brought over a towel that we had wet with cool water, and took off her heavy work boots, which were covered with thick mud. We gently removed the clothes that were stuck to her body and wiped her arms and face with the towel. Her body was lax, and she didn't say a word. Like a good little girl, she lifted one hand, and then the other, as we slipped on her pajamas.

Then we combed her hair, and only after she was clean and dressed for the night that had already ended did we sit her up and pile our pillows behind her back. Now that she was sitting on her bed, Ayala pleaded with her, "Eat." But Mira didn't touch the food. Ayala sat down next to her and buttered a slice of bread, broke it in half, sliced it into little pieces, and then she brought it to Mira's mouth in a teaspoon. Slowly, slowly, and with great patience, as if she were feeding a little girl.

After Mira had eaten a little, and seemed to have recovered some of her strength, she said, "They're not my parents, they're not." We calmed her and said that she didn't have to talk now, despite the fact that we were

dying of curiosity. "I want you to know," she said,
"they're not my parents. They are horrible people." We
looked at one another, and then we looked at her. She
stopped talking, sipped a little from the cup of tea that
was sitting in front of her, and then pushed the tray away.
Ayala took it from her. Then, Mira sat upright, leaned her
back against the pillows, caressed the blanket with her
hands, and after a long silence, said, "They clung to me
already in Naples, in Italy. I remember it as if it were
today. We arrived there in a Polish boat, together with a
lot of other kids."

Chavi asked, "Where are you from in Poland?"

"I don't exactly know. I don't remember anything,"
Mira said. "I only remember the Polish children's home.
They brought us there after the war. I don't know who
brought me. I don't know how long I was there at the
children's home in Poland. Until one day, they put us on
this ship, and they said, 'You're going to Israel.' "

Chavi and Esty asked, "Where was this children's
home? In which city in Poland? We're also from there."

"A city, I just don't know, but the children's home
was called *Dom Zetzki* which means The Children's
Home."

Then Esty said, "All the children's homes are called
dom zetzki or *dom zeitzi*. We were also in a *dom*, but ours
was called *Dom Zeitzi Jerusalem*. Don't you remember
what your *dom* was called?"

"I just remember that I felt good there," Mira said.
"There were people who taught us to speak and sing a

little in Hebrew, until we left the place. When we
reached Naples—"

A knock on the door interrupted her. Ariel came in
and said in a whisper, "Girls, the guards say that they saw
someone running through the fields toward the youth
village."

"Ariel, she's here," Chavi said. He breathed a tremendous sigh of relief.

"Do you mind if Ariel sits here and listens to your
story?" Esty asked Mira.

Ariel said, "First of all, I want you to know that I'm
happy that you're here, Mira. Your friends and I were
really so worried about you. I also want you to know
that I trusted you. I knew that you would return."

Mira didn't react. She just looked at him, and the old
evil seemed to be gone from her eyes.

She continued where she had left off. "Then, when
we got to Italy, to Naples, some older people got on the
ship. Each one took a child and said it was his, or that he
was a close relative. And me too, I was found by those
people. I'm sure that they were the ones who came to
look for me today. They told me on the ship that those
were my parents and that they had been looking for me
throughout the war. Those people hugged me and took
me from the ship. They bought me some really nice
clothing," she added, "and a big doll with curly hair that
opened and closed its eyes. I stayed with them for a few
days in Naples, and then afterward, we got on another
ship and came to Israel."

Ariel sat there listening, just like us. We didn't interrupt her, and she kept on talking. "All the time I had this
feeling that they weren't my parents. At first, after we
arrived in Israel, they were okay. We lived in Afula, in a
little house in an immigrant neighborhood. The man had
work, I went to school, and everything was normal. I
called them 'Mother' and 'Father,' even though I knew it
wasn't true, but I didn't say anything. One day the man
got fired. He never found another job, and she got sick.
And then he began to loaf around, to drink, to go wild
in the house, and to bother me. He began to get angry
with me, to shout and to hit..." And again Mira was
silent. Then, as if she were gathering her strength, she said,
"When they began to mistreat me, I couldn't stand it any
longer, and I ran away. My whole back was filled with
marks and scars from their blows, mainly from him."

I almost said, "Yes, yes. I saw the scars on her back,"
but I was silent.

"So I ran away," Mira continued. "I ran away from
them three years ago. They didn't even look for me. They
knew exactly where I was. The social worker who
helped me run away told them that I was at the *Masuot*
youth village, but they didn't visit me even once. Why
did they suddenly come today? If I see them, I could kill
them." Once again, that harsh look returned to Mira's
face. Hatred overwhelmed her, and her eyes were once
more filled with evil.

After a long silence, Ariel said, "I want to understand
something, Mira. When you say 'I knew that something

was wrong, that they weren't my parents,' what do you mean?"

Ayala volunteered to explain. She said, "Ariel, she doesn't remember anything about what happened to her before she met them. She doesn't remember where she comes from."

Ariel said gently, "Thank you, Ayala. But Mira can explain."

"I don't know," Mira said. "I don't remember anything. I don't know who my parents were, what they looked like, where I was before the war and during the war itself, and how I survived. Sometimes I try to remember, I want to, but I can't. I can't remember anything. It's as if my memory were taken from me and I was left with nothing."

The room was already flooded with the morning spring light that came in through the window, and I heard the other girls on their way to the shower room. We listened to the noise, looked at one another, and laughed. "Is that what we sound like in the morning, like a flock of geese?" And Ariel said yes. Afterward he suggested that we stay behind and rest a while after our long night. He wanted to release us from our morning work assignments, but we refused. At the youth village we had been taught the importance of work, and we couldn't imagine evading our responsibilities just because we had stayed up all night. "What's so hard about three hours of work, Ariel? The worst that can happen is that we'll go to sleep early tonight."

Before Ariel left our room, he said, "Mira, I want you to know we're here for you, and anything you need from us, we'll do. You can be certain that no one will harm you."

Mira said, quietly, "I know that. Now I know that."

A few days went by, and they appeared once again: the man and the woman. We were sitting on the grass opposite the dining room when they arrived. The sun was setting, intoxicating fragrances of spring were in the air, and the sky looked as if it were painted red. I was sitting there, leaning against Yurek's back, and I felt good. When I saw them approaching, I quietly said to Mira, "Mira, look. It's them." And before I finished the sentence, once again, she jumped up and ran away like mad, practically trampling over some of the kids. Everyone was really surprised and didn't understand what was happening. It all happened so fast.

Ariel got up and immediately started to run after her. He managed to catch up to her, and from afar we saw him leading her to the building where he lived. He came back alone. The man and the woman passed us and continued on toward the group's quarters. Ariel followed, and soon caught up with them. We didn't hear what they said to each other, but a few minutes later, we heard shouts coming from the direction of our rooms and saw the man swinging his hands around and his wife dragging after him. "It's a scandal," he shouted. "They don't let us see our child. What's going on here? Are these a bunch of Nazis who steal kids from their parents?" The man threatened to call the police.

Ariel stood in front of us, and said, "Gang, I'll explain what happened later. Just stay in your places."

The man came toward us and screamed with all his might, "Mira Segal, I want Mira Segal here, right now! I'm her father. Mira Segal is my child. This is my wife. We want to see Mira." We didn't say a word and didn't reveal where she was. The other kids were shocked, since they had no idea what was going on. We hadn't told anyone that these two had been here once before and that Mira had run away. Now they understood what she was running away from.

Ariel said to the man, "I'm asking you, mister, leave this place quietly, and don't make a fuss. She doesn't want to see you. If she wanted to, she'd be here."

The man kept screaming, "Mira!" and his face looked really horrible.

The little woman at his side said, "He's got a bad heart. He's sick from the war, from the Germans. The doctors say he mustn't get angry. Bring our girl to us." The kids who had been on their way to the dining room came over and surrounded them. When the two realized that it was a lost cause, that Mira wouldn't come out to them, they started heading toward the gate.

Supper was shorter than ever, and afterward we all went to Ariel's room. We sat crowded together on his mat, and Mira was among us. We really loved that room. Ariel collected books and records, and we sat there qui-

etly listening to the sounds of Brahms' Concerto for
Violin and Cello. Only Sarah B. moved her body to the
sound of the music, conducting the orchestra with her
beautiful fingers. It was good. It was as if a warm current
connected all of our bodies. We knew that when we
were together in that room, no harm could befall us,
none of us would get hurt.

And when the sounds of the violin and the cello died
down, we all listened to the news. The radio in Ariel's
room was our window to the great wide world, to the
country, to everything that was outside of our youth village. In that evening's news broadcast, the commentator
reported in his dramatic voice about the demonstrations
that were taking place throughout the country against
the reparations from Germany. Toward the end of the
broadcast, the commentator said that "the search contin-
ues for the unknown assailant who hit the great violinist
Jascha Heifetz on the hand, in front of his Jerusalem
hotel, after he played a sonata by Richard Strauss." Ariel
explained that Richard Strauss was a German composer
who had been known for his admiration and support for
the Nazi regime during the first years of its existence.

"It's strange," Chavi said, "that such a great Jewish
artist would play a work by Richard Strauss, here, in
Israel."

We spoke about art and artists and about freedom of
expression. We tried to decide whether music should be
judged by quality alone, or whether it should also be
considered in other contexts—for example, political

ones—and when, if and why art should be censored.

The spirit of the discussion was very positive. I loved those talks about things that were beyond the daily life of our village. Ariel knew how to draw us after him and to guide us; he wanted us to be aware of things outside. "This is not the center of the world," he would say. "We live here, this is our home, but the world is there on the other side of the road." And when we had these discussions in Ariel's room, even the tone of our conversation was different. "Look how we're talking, like older, cultured people. It's a real pleasure to be with you," Ariel would say. And at the end of that discussion, the majority agreed that it was forbidden to play even one note from a work by an artist who admired the Nazis, no matter how great he was, not here, not on this land, in this country. It was forbidden!

Zevick wanted to say something, and Ayala glared at him with her big black eyes. This time, he didn't shout, he spoke. "As for me," he said, "if it were up to me, I'd beat this Jascha Heifetz with both my hands."

During the next few days, we made a special effort to take care of Mira. She was afraid to be alone, even for a minute. We were always there, together with her. Mira, who was so independent, who never asked for anything from anyone, now said, "Don't leave me alone, I'm afraid they'll come back."

A week later, when it was Mira's turn to take care of the room, we found it cleaned and aired out: fresh flow-

ers were in the vases, and all the mail was in the right
places. Long letters had arrived from our friend Dita in
America. She had a new boyfriend. They won first prize
in a dance contest at their school. Her mother was preg-
nant from her new husband. Dita wrote all sorts of little
descriptions about her new life in America. She wrote an
almost identical letter to each one of us. And the letters
were there, waiting for us, standing like little soldiers in
the drawers, so that we wouldn't miss them.

Mira's bed, which was always left out in the middle
of the room during the day, was now in its proper place
under Ayala's bed, folded away from view. Once again,
our room was beautiful and well taken care of, the way
it had been in the days before Mira's arrival at the youth
village. We didn't say a word to her. It was clear to us that
this was the way to react. And now, we knew that she
had finally become one of us. Every evening we orga-
nized defensive measures, just in case the people claiming
to be her parents would carry out their threat to return.
They would "blow up the village," they had said. We
weren't worried about explosives, we were worried
about Mira. "They're capable of doing anything," said
Mira. "He's got friends, real ruffians, all of Afula was
afraid of them." The heads of the youth village listened
to Mira and alerted the police to the possibility that
something might happen.

An order was given to turn on all the huge lights that
surrounded the youth village at night, so that the courtyard would be flooded with light. Musa, who was

responsible for guarding the village, periodically checked the area around our quarters, riding around on his horse. And while we were still awake, we went out to visit him, wrapped in blankets, joking with him and playing with Horsey, his big, lovable dog.

Mira said, "Look at what I'm doing to your lives. All these problems. Do you really need me here?"

And it was easy for us to answer. "We all have our problems, and each of us has her difficult moments and her little joys. So right now, it's your problems that have center stage," Ayala said. Mira listened to us and laughed, a real genuine laugh. We had never heard her laugh before.

Those two people never returned to the youth village, but we heard that they turned to the courts. They sued the youth village for illegally holding their daughter. And they demanded that Mira be returned home to them immediately. "They want a trial? Let them have a trial," Mira said.

CHAPTER 12

One afternoon Ariel told us the latest news about Mira's case. Then he turned toward her and asked, "Mira, do you want us to talk about this, here, in front of everyone?"

"Yes, definitely. It's really important for me to know what all of you think. I want us to talk about it," Mira said.

Yurek said, "I want to understand exactly what they want, these people who claim to be your parents."

"Me," Mira said, "They want me back."

"Why aren't you with them?" Zevick asked. "After all, you've got a home, and parents."

But Mira wouldn't budge. Once again, the harsh evil look returned to her eyes. "No, Zevick. I have no home and no parents. It's one big lie. They are not my parents. You've got to believe me." She looked at us when she spoke. "You already know me a little. I can be terrible. But with them, in their home, it was really horrible. I felt that I was capable of doing the most awful things to them. Whole nights I used to dream that I was murdering them, and that really frightened me. It's already three years since I left them. Where were they all this time? Why did they suddenly remember me now? What do they want from me? I wish I knew."

I listened to Mira's words and looked at the kids. I surveyed the faces of my friends, one by one, and I thought, *How strange. After all, the dream of everyone who is sitting here is to one day find a relative, a lost parent, a father, a mother.* And for Mira, two people show up, parents, and they say, "You're ours, come home," and she runs away from them.

Ayala said, "Maybe they think that you're already old enough to take care of them."

"Maybe they want you to go to work for them, to support them, to make money. In the city, there are a lot of workers our age," Daniel suggested. Yes, even Daniel, who couldn't stand looking at her face or hearing her voice, even he cared about her, just like the rest of us.

And then Yurek said, "I don't know how to put it, but I think there's a connection between their visit and the reparations from Germany. Maybe they think that they can get the money that's coming to you. Maybe that's the reason that they suddenly want you."

"I don't care what the reason is," Mira said. "I'm never in my life going back to those people. I know they're not my parents. The trouble is, I don't know who my real parents are. But I'll fight for my right not to return to them."

After those words, there was silence. No one said a word. Mira looked at us, hoping for some warmth and encouragement. Yurek cleared his throat, and said, "Gang, we've got to help Mira in this struggle. This could happen to any one of us. Just try to imagine someone trying to take advantage of one of us, claiming that he or she is your or my father or mother. It's a fight for our right to be ourselves, and I suggest that if there's a trial—"

Before he had a chance to finish, Ariel cut in. "There will be a trial, Yurek, and a date has already been set for when Mira has to appear in court."

Now it was even easier for Yurek to say, without sounding sentimental, "If that's so, then, Mira, you won't be alone there. I suggest that we all go to the courthouse." But then Ariel said that we wouldn't be allowed to be present at the trial, because it would be held behind closed doors.

Sarah B., in her typical know-it-all manner, said, "Well, of course. She's underage. She isn't seventeen yet." And once again, I was amazed. *Where does she pick up all this knowledge? Where does she get it from?* I wondered.

Ariel confirmed what Sarah B. had said. "To my regret, we won't be able to be there with you, Mira, but the youth village has already appointed a lawyer who will represent us in the trial. She's going to arrive tomorrow, and she'll meet with Mira and with us. Tomorrow, we'll all be wiser. But one thing's certain, Mira, in this trial: Just as Yurek said, you're not alone; we're all with you. It will be as if each and every one of us were standing before the judge and you were just chosen to be our representative."

The next day, the lawyer arrived. She appeared in the dining room, accompanied by Rachel. Ariel got up to greet her and shake the hand of the young woman. Then he introduced her to us. "Gang," he said, "please meet attorney Ofra Eilam."

And Rachel said to us, "I understand that you already know about the trial that will soon take place." Then she turned to the lawyer. "In order to reassure you, I want to explain that we don't keep any children here by force. Everything is legal and in order. To our great sorrow, most of the children here are orphaned from their parents, without a family. And in this home, in this great family that we have established, everyone is here on a voluntary basis, in accordance with the law. But, of course, we must find out if there is any basis to those people's claim, to make sure that this isn't a case of misunderstanding between parents and their daughter. And we know that such disagreements between parents and their children happen quite frequently during the teenage years."

Mira, who was squirming in her seat, just couldn't contain herself. "Rachel, I swear to you, they are not my parents, they're lying. It's all one big lie. They're trying to take advantage of me."

"Try to be calm," said Rachel. "This isn't the time or place to talk about it. Come to my house after supper, and the three of us—you, me, and our lawyer—will talk

about it. You know that we'll listen to you and do everything we can to help you." Then she called Mira over
and introduced her to Ofra. To us she said, "Ofra Eilam
will be spending some time with you, and I hope that
you'll all cooperate with her and answer her questions,
so that we can help her provide legal support to Mira."

Rachel left, and Ariel arranged for Ofra to join our
vegetarian table, the only one with empty chairs. We
carefully examined this young, confident woman. She
looked very youthful, with her short hair and clothes
that sat neatly on her slim body. She carried a big, brown
leather briefcase, which was packed with papers. During
the meal, we noticed that Ariel was drawn toward our
table, and every so often he would say something to her
or to us. Eventually he made his way to our table and sat
down to eat with us.

Ofra had a warm, deep voice. She asked questions
about the youth village, about our life here, but didn't say
a word about Mira or the trial. Only later, when we sat
around her in the activity room, did she explain about
the trial, what she expected would happen there, and
what she wanted from us.

During the next few days, Ofra Eilam spent a lot of
time with us. She would arrive at the youth village in the
afternoon, and we would wait for her, together with
Mira, at the gate. Mira was always happy to see her, and
we were, too. Almost every day, we had a visitor from the
outside world.

The first session of the court on Mira's matter was set

for Sunday morning at eight o'clock in the big city of
Tel Aviv. The group decided by unanimous decision that
a delegation of two people would accompany Mira to
the courthouse. The delegates for the first session were
Yurek and I.

So, at exactly six o'clock on Sunday morning, Ariel
came to wake Mira and me up, with his familiar light
knock on the door. All the girls in the room were already
up and dressed. We practically hadn't slept a wink all
night. Mira sat on her bed and hardly spoke. We were
there, ready to listen to her if she had anything to say or
to help her if she needed any help. But she was silent.
And when morning broke, she was dressed and ready to
go. We followed her example. We got dressed and
washed, as if we were all joining her on the journey.

Yurek joined us at the entrance to the dining room.
As always, he stretched his hand out to greet me, and I
blushed. The dining room, which was already set the
night before, looked big and abandoned without the rest
of the kids. There was complete silence. Mira barely
touched her food. She just sat there, wearing her blue
farmer's cap. I wanted to tell her that it wasn't necessary,
to take it off. But when I saw the expression on her face
that morning, it reminded me of how she looked the
first time we met, and I held back. Most of the time, she
just sat there, her face turned toward the window, hidden
by her cap. I didn't know what she saw, but the tight
movement of her lips revealed how tense she was.

On the way out of the dining room, Ariel rested his

hand on Mira's shoulder, and to my surprise, she didn't remove it. They left that way, together, until we reached the gate.

Armed with sandwiches and a thermos filled with tea, we climbed onto the pickup truck that would take us to the courthouse in the big city. The girls waved to us and shouted, "You'll win, Mira, you've got to win." Musa drove the truck. The three of us sat in the back, the cool morning wind beating against our faces, and we hardly said a word.

Suddenly Mira said, "Tell Musa to stop. Hurry. I don't feel well." Yurek hit the back of the cabin, and Musa stopped. Mira climbed down to the side of the road and began to vomit. I moved toward her, wanting to help. "Don't come too close," she said. "There's no need. I'll manage." We stood there, not far from her, feeling helpless. Afterward, she wiped her face with a handkerchief that was in her pocket, breathed some fresh air into her lungs, put the cap back on her head, climbed back up onto the truck, and said, "I'm fine now." And she added, "It must have been something that I ate." But we knew that she had barely touched the food and understood that it was the excitement that she was feeling.

We passed through the streets of the awakening city. The stores were opening right before our eyes, and tons of kids filled the sidewalks on their way to school. I wanted to stop the truck, to get off, and to disappear among them. To leave my home for school in the morning and to return home in the afternoon, just like them.

Ofra Eilam was at the entrance to the courthouse, impatiently waiting for Mira. She was wearing a dark suit, a white blouse that was buttoned up to her neck, and a dark ribbon tie. She looked much older than she had at our youth village. Before we entered the lobby of the courthouse, Ofra said, "Mira, take off your cap."

"No, I like it," Mira objected.

But Ofra wouldn't give in. "You've got nothing to hide. You have a pretty face. That stupid cap makes you look ridiculous." Mira obeyed, took the cap off, and put it on my head. I made a face, coiled my tongue, and crossed my eyes to make her laugh. And for the first time since yesterday evening, the hint of a smile appeared on Mira's lips.

The courtroom door closed behind them, and Yurek and I were left outside, together, far away from the group—just me and him in a big, strange city, waiting for our friend who was struggling for the right to remain an orphan.

Mira traveled three times to the courthouse in the big city. And each time she was accompanied by two members of the group, a boy and a girl, armed with sandwiches and a thermos filled with hot tea. Despite the fact that the trial took place behind closed doors, we knew almost everything that happened on the other side of that big door. When Mira and the delegation returned to the youth village, we would gather around her to hear about the trial. We insisted that she not leave out a single detail. We wanted to know everything. "Fear... tremen-

dous fear...I was so afraid...what fear"—those words
appeared over and over again in Mira's stories. "You can't
imagine how afraid I was today," she said one day. "They
brought a witness who told the judge that he was with
the Segals in the ghetto, and he remembers that they had
a little girl, about four or five years old, and according to
his calculation, she should be big now. 'About this girl's
age,' he said, pointing at me. And I don't remember being
in a ghetto at all. I felt frightened to death of this man."
We wanted to know how the judge reacted, but Mira
didn't know what to say. "He almost never says anything,
just listens," she said. "And from his face, it's hard to tell
what he's thinking."

Everything connected to the court frightened Mira.
Police cars with bars on their windows that brought
prisoners to the courthouse and policemen who walked
in and out of the building aroused her fears as if she were
still a little girl. "Policemen frighten me," she said. "I see
uniforms and I'm immediately scared to death." She
looked at us, a little confused. "I know that it's stupid. But
it's a fact, I'm frightened."

Only on the day that Rena Yahezkieli took the witness stand did Mira calm down a little. Rena Yehezkieli
was the social worker from Afula who had helped Mira
run away from home, and Ofra brought her to bear witness. She told the judge the truth about those people,
about the blows, and how she had helped Mira escape
from them. Mira filled us in when she got home. "She
told the judge what I told you, that they knew where I

was and weren't interested in me for three whole years.
That during all the years I was at the Masuot youth village, they totally ignored me. Ofra said that Rena
Yehezkieli's testimony was very important and that it
would help us."

The group decided that for the final decisive session,
all of us would accompany Mira to the courthouse. We
were released from work and classes so that we could all
go together with her to Tel Aviv. And in the morning of
that day, in the midst of all the hustle and bustle, Yola
came into the shower room carrying a hanger with the
new clothes we had prepared for her trip to Poland: the
white blouse with the blue and red embroidery, the blue
A-line skirt, and the Tiberias belt. And when she came
in, she said, "Mira, I'd like you to wear these clothes
today at the courthouse. It's an important day, and you
should dress nicely. You'll be beautiful in these clothes."

Mira, who was leaning over the sink, stood up, looked
at her with astonishment, and then looked at us, but she
didn't dare touch the clothes. We were just as surprised
as she was. And suddenly there was complete silence in
the shower room.

Then Yola said, "Tell her, girls, tell her to wear them.
They're new, I never wore them even once." We were
silent. Again Yola pleaded, "Do it for me, I want you to.
Please." Mira didn't move. She just stood there, with her
washing kit in one hand, a towel hanging over the other,
and both hands seem to have been frozen like a statue.
Yola removed the blouse and the skirt from the hanger.

"Come on, put them on, I'll help you," she said, and she took the washing kit and the towel from Mira's hands. Mira gave in and let Yola dress her, as if she were a little obedient girl. Afterward Yola combed her hair. Mira looked really pretty, almost beautiful. The clothes really suited her. Yola prepared her for the trip to the court-house just the way we had prepared her for the journey to Poland.

CHAPTER 13

Ofra Eilam and her assistant were waiting for us outside the courthouse. "I spoke with the judge," said Ofra, "and as a special gesture, he's going to let all of you be present in the courtroom." We shouted with joy, but Ofra immediately quieted us down. "There are very severe regulations here, and we must abide by them. When the bailiff calls the court to order, you must all stand up and wait until the judge enters the courtroom. Only after the judge sits down are you allowed to sit. And from that moment on, only silence. You mustn't talk or react. Even if you feel a tremendous desire to participate or help your friend, you must remain spectators, silent observers. And keep this in mind," she said, "any noise, even the slightest disturbance by any of you, and you'll all be sent outside. Understood?" And then we went inside. The transition from the bright morning sunlight to the gray courtroom, with its naked, shoddy walls, was very harsh. Sitting there, I felt as if it were a dark rainy day, not the beginning of summer.

Besides the national emblem, which hung on the wall
behind the judge's chair, the walls were completely
naked. The courtroom looked sad and pitiful. For some
reason, I had imagined that, behind the big door, I would
discover a very elegant hall, which would suit a place that
determined people's fates.

Mira, Ofra, and her apprentice, Eitan, were sitting to
our right on a wooden bench in the first row. Opposite
them, on the left side of the courtroom, sat Mr. and Mrs.
Segal and their lawyer. The bailiff called the court to order
in a loud exaggerated voice, which didn't quite fit the rel-
atively small courtroom. The judge entered, wearing a
black cloak. Without any special mannerisms, he sat down
on his high chair on the stage in front of the court. The
judge looked around and turned toward Mr. and Mrs.
Segal. Relying on the testimony of Rena Yehezkieli, the
social worker from Afula who had described all of the difficulties and problems in the Segal house until Mira had
left, the judge asked, "Why are you, who have known such
pain and sorrow in your lives, insisting that she come
home? I would like to understand this better, to know
more," he said. "After all, if she's your daughter and she's
happy in the place where she's living, why don't you let
her stay there? You can visit her every so often and renew
your ties on a healthier basis—slowly, without pressure.
The girl says that she feels good at this youth village." Then
the judge looked at us and added, "Look, she's surrounded here by friends who love her, who came here to be
with her during this difficult time. This means something."

The Segals' lawyer got up and said, "Your Honor, Mira should be with her parents. Their hearts are breaking because of the distance between them. As parents," he said, "their wish is to see her get married, raise a family, have children. Only then will they be able to relax a little, after everything they have gone through in their lives. After that terrible war that left them broken, both in body and soul."

Mira broke in, "That can't be what they want. They're not my parents. They know just as well as I do that they're not my parents."

The judge asked Ofra to calm her and asked Mira not to make any more outbursts. Then he suggested to Mr. Segal and to Mira that they undergo a blood test, and he emphasized that such a test can only indicate that someone isn't one's father. It can't prove that he is the father. "This blood test," he said, "could help us to move forward in our search for a solution to this difficult problem that we're dealing with."

When Mr. Segal heard this, he began to shout, "They don't trust Jews here. What people! As if the Germans didn't carry out enough experiments on us." He took off his jacket, rolled up his shirt sleeve, and exposed a thin, white veiny arm with a blue number branded on it. "Isn't that enough?" he shouted. "Auschwitz wasn't enough? And why all the fuss? Just because a father and a mother want their daughter back?"

His tiny wife followed his example. "I also have the same thing," she shouted. "Look," she said, rolling up her

sleeve. "This is from Hitler. There is no place on my body
where they didn't stab me or cut me. Isn't that enough?
Isn't there any justice here?"

Her husband tried to get her to sit down. Then he
shouted, "No tests, no blood. I just want my child!" Mira
looked with fear at the judge, looked at Ofra, and for the
first time, looked at us, as if maybe we could help.

Silence settled over the courtroom, with only the
clicking of a neon light making a sound like a cricket
that had snuck into the building. The judge turned
toward Mira. He spoke in a quiet, friendly voice.
"Young lady," he said, "maybe, despite all your feelings,
you can try to return home for a trial period? A home
is a home. Do you know how many children are homeless?"

And then Ofra Eilam asked for the right to speak. She
explained that only now, after three years away from
home, had Mira begun to recover. Yet the judge continued to pressure her. He left his seat and stood very close
to Mira; he almost breathed on her when he said, "All
this time you have claimed 'They're not my parents,
they're not!' So who are your parents? Tell the court who
your parents are. After all, you still haven't said anything
about this." He continued to stand there, close to her,
waiting for her to say something.

We were crowded together on the benches, so close
to one another that we felt as if we were one body. We
thought, *Say something, try to remember, give a sign.* We tried
with all our might to transfer our thoughts to her since

we had been forbidden to speak, either to her or among ourselves.

The judge was very patient. He leaned toward her and said, "We have time, young lady. No one wants to hurry you. Try to remember something, about your mother, your father, a brother, a sister. If these people aren't your parents, then who are your parents?"

Mira looked at him and whispered, "I just don't remember anything. I don't know."

"But, young lady," said the judge, "you must understand. These people claim that they're your parents. If they're wrong, I have to know why they're wrong. Make an effort, try to remember a detail, a bit of information, something."

Mira looked at the two people who were sitting on the bench, she stared and stared, and then she said, "I think they were taller... that's what I think." The words came out of her mouth, broken and hesitant.

The judge, who had returned to his high chair overlooking the courtroom, stood up and said, "My dear, am I tall or short?" Mira just looked at him and was silent. "I'm a short man," he said, "everyone would agree to that. But when my children were very young, they thought I was a big and tall father. You were a very young girl, and you looked at your mother from here," he said, indicating the height of a small girl with his hand. But Mira didn't give up. It was clear that she was mobilizing all of her strength to try to remember. The judge sat on his chair, folded his arms, and waited.

"Think for a moment, young lady," he said. "Here are
two people in front of you, who want what is best for
you. You heard them say that they want to see you raise
a family here in Israel. After everything they went
through, why don't you return home?"

Mira blurted out, "No. It's better to die."

Ofra turned toward the judge and asked for permission to talk with Mira, quietly. We didn't hear what she
said to her. She spoke to her in a whisper, and Mira
shook her head no.

The couple's lawyer got up, and with the judge's permission, he said, "Your Honor, the picture is clear. After
we have been sitting here for such a long time, if the girl
still can't present even one point that contradicts her parents' words, I think that she should return home. That's
the best thing for everyone concerned." The woman
wiped her nose, wiped away some tears, and busied herself with her purse, as if she were trying to revive her
spirits. And the lawyer added, "Look, Your Honor, at the
pain in my client's face: She's lost her strength to sit here.
The woman is a Holocaust survivor. She's very sick. Her
husband is also a sick man. This incident in their lives,
this nightmare, must come to an end as soon as possible.
I'm very worried about both of them." He thanked the
judge and returned to his seat.

Once again, the judge looked at Mira. He turned
toward Ofra Eilam and said, "Madam, we must move forward, and not particularly because of the last words of
the learned lawyer. I see no alternative but to…"

Suddenly we heard Mira mumbling, "Blue...blue."

The judge said, "I can't hear you, young lady. Please speak a little louder."

Mira ignored his words, and continued, "Blue, blue, I remember blue." Silence reigned over the courtroom. Everything froze.

Ofra leaned over toward Mira and said, "What was blue, Mira? What was blue?"

"I remember blue. When I was here," and she gently raised her hands as if she were cradling a baby between them. She said, "When I was here, like this. I used to look upward and see blue. She had blue eyes, I remember, really blue. And she had long black eyelashes, like butter-flies, on her eyes. A lot of black eyelashes. And when she would look down at me, it was as if a shadow had fallen on her white face. She had a pale face, and she had a beauty mark, yes, a beauty mark, here," and she pointed to her face, touching the spot where her mother had this beauty mark. "A little above her upper lip, here. And above her chin, she had a dimple, right here." Her finger moved over her face and stopped in the center of her chin. "Right here, she had a dimple, I remember. I...I see her face," she cried. "I see my mother, my beautiful mother. How come I couldn't see her until now?" she cried, as if she were a blind person who had just begun to see. Tears flooded down her face.

We sat there without saying a word, secretly holding hands. Ofra looked at us, and we could see that her eyes were wet. Mira continued, "She had teeth that stood out

slightly. Her front tooth was sort of funny." Mira moved
her hand toward her open mouth, revealing her teeth.
"Yes, yes, just like me. That's what my mother was like.
And my brother also had teeth like that." For the first
time, we heard that she had a brother. "Antek, his name
was Antek. My brother, Antek Rozner. And my mother
was Hela Rozner, and my father, Menahem Rozner.
Rozner, our name is Rozner." And she repeated,
"Rozner, Miriam Rozner. I'm Miriam Rozner. I lived in
Ulica Lubertowska, Lublin. Yes, that's it, Lublin. Miriam
Rozner, not Segal. They're Segal, not me."

It seemed as if saying the forgotten names of her family brought her back to the courtroom. "I want my
name," she said, "I want to be what I really am, Your
Honor, I want you to help me be Miriam Rozner from
Poland. I know exactly who I am now. How could I have
forgotten my mother, my father, and my brother,
Antek?" she said. "I so wanted to remember, and I just
wasn't able to. How did this happen?" Her voice grew
weak and she burst into a loud sob.

Mira—who never cried, ever—totally collapsed; she
just seemed to break down completely. Ofra supported
her and hugged her. We saw her wipe away Mira's tears
and caress her face. The judge, who tried to remain calm,
removed his glasses, closed his eyes, buried his face in his
hands, and was silent for what seemed like a long, long
time. We all waited for him to say something.

Mr. and Mrs. Segal just sat there, drooped in their
places, and it was clear that they felt very uncomfortable.

The tiny woman seemed to have shrunk even more, and the man sitting next to her bit his lips, not exchanging a word with her.

The judge called for a recess. The bailiff called out in his thundering voice, "The court will rise," and we all stood still until the judge left the courtroom. As soon as he left, we rushed over to Mira and surrounded her. "Miriam Rozner," we cried out, "Miriam Rozner," and we hugged her. All the words, all the sounds that we had held back during the trial burst forth in a tremendous flow of happiness and emotion. We didn't even notice that half an hour had passed by. And when the bailiff shouted out again, "The court will rise," we all ran back to our places. We stood there, very tense, trying to guess the judge's decision by his facial expressions.

The judge talked about that terrible war and its many victims, about the pain that would never end, and the wound that would never heal. He spoke to Mr. and Mrs. Segal with warmth and understanding, and we were afraid that he was going to hand Mira over to them. He explained that even if they were Mira's biological parents, he would release her from them, because she was almost an adult and it was wrong to impose a home that she didn't want to live in. His words expressed the pain he felt about the loneliness that awaited them when they returned home. His pain about the child they lost in the war. "But one child cannot replace another one," said the judge. And then he turned toward Mira. "My young lady," he said. "With the coming of memory, I would like

---

to ask all of your teachers and counselors at the youth village to help you in every way possible. Maybe, some day, someone close to you, a relative, will be found, someone who is looking for you, waiting for you. Everything possible should be done to ensure that you can once again be Miriam Rozner, the daughter of Menahem and Hela Rozner from Lublin." He added, "And now, go to your friends, and live your life, and don't be angry at these two people."

The judge left the courtroom. He was followed by Mr. and Mrs. Segal, who were accompanied by their lawyer. On their way out, they stopped for a moment. Maybe they wanted to say something to Mira, but they didn't dare approach our circle that surrounded and protected her. We just stood there, really close to one another, embracing and feeling a real sense of togetherness, through good and bad. It was a wonderful moment, and we didn't want it to end.

Ofra Eilam came toward us, without the black cloak that she wore throughout the trial. Dressed only in her white blouse and dark skirt, she once again looked very young. We were really thankful for what she had done for our Mira and poured out our love to her. Ariel hugged Ofra, and for a moment, she remained in his arms. Afterward, she released herself and put her arms around his shoulders. The two of them stood really close to each other, and they looked so beautiful together.

Mira, who never showed any signs of affection toward anyone, hugged and kissed Ofra. We literally took over the sidewalk outside the courthouse, and people passing by saw the joy in our faces. Our happiness seemed to be contagious, because they said, "What wonderful youth, these kids."

There was a falafel stand on the street corner. Falafel was our national dish. We really love those little mashed, deep-fried chickpea balls, with their delicious spices. All we had to do was say the word "falafel" and our taste buds would begin to work overtime. However, since there was no falafel at the youth village, we could only dream about every so often visiting a town or city where we could have a falafel sandwich in a pita bread.

Nearby stood a bored-looking street photographer with a huge camera, waiting for customers. Ariel called out to Mira, "Miriam Rozner, come here. Let's preserve your new face for eternity." She had her picture taken, alone, and then we all joined in for a group picture. Afterward, Ariel invited all of us to have a falafel at the corner stand. "This is the best falafel in the country," said Ariel.

Only Sarah B. refused to eat. "It's vulgar," she said, "to eat in the street. I can wait." Her reaction made us laugh, but we didn't mock her; we just laughed in good spirits.

Before we climbed onto the truck that would take us back to our youth village, we stopped by the street photographer to pick up the pictures. On the back of the group picture, Ariel wrote: "Miriam Rozner and her good friends, Tel Aviv, 1953."

Only after the truck had left the big city did Yurek

lean over to me and whisper, "Listen, when the truck comes close to the village and passes near the hill, I'll knock on the back of the cabin so that Musa will stop. We'll both get off quickly and run to the domim tree to celebrate a little on our own." We held hands during the entire trip. Every so often, I looked at Yurek. He almost looked like a native Israeli as he always wanted to, even without a rolling *resh* and with his foreign mannerisms. I loved him so much just the way he was.

We sang all the way from the big city to the youth village—song after song. We were really hoarse, and Mira was the only one who didn't join in. Her lips moved with the songs, but there was no sound. She sat there among us, squeezed inside the truck, dressed in Yola's beautiful traveling clothes, exposing her face to the wind. Her hair was loose in a wild dance. And she was holding her blue cap in her hands, fondling it.

When the truck turned from the main road toward the path that led to the youth village, "The Dutch Hill" suddenly appeared in all its splendor. The truck stopped. Someone had beaten us to it, had already knocked on the driver's cabin. We saw Mira jump down from the truck and race toward the hill. She ran so fast, waving her cap at us, like someone was waiting for her at the top of the hill. Then she turned her back toward us, and we accompanied her with our eyes as she neared the top of the path leading toward the domim tree. Yurek turned to me and smiled. "We can't go up now. The domim tree is taken."